KEYNOTES

KEYNOTES

BY
GEORGE EGERTON

ISBN: 978-93-5128-365-2(HB)

First Published in 1893
Indian Reprint in 2017

Published by

Kalpaz Publications
C-30, Satyawati Nagar,
Delhi – 110052
E-mail: kalpaz@hotmail.com
Website: kalpazpublications.com
Ph.: +91-9212142040

CONTENTS

A CROSS LINE

THE rather flat notes of a man's voice float out into the clear air, singing the refrain of a popular music-hall ditty. There is something incongruous between the melody and the surroundings. It seems profane, indelicate, to bring this slangy, vulgar tune, and with it the mental picture of footlight flare and fantastic dance into the lovely freshness of this perfect spring day.

A woman sitting on a felled tree turns her head to meet its coming, and an expression flits across her face in which disgust and humorous appreciation are subtly blended. Her mind is nothing if not picturesque ; her busy brain, with all its capabilities choked by a thousand vagrant fancies, is always producing pictures and finding associations between the most unlikely objects. She has been reading a little sketch written in the daintiest language of a fountain scene in Tanagra, and her vivid imagination has made it real to her. The slim, graceful maids grouped around it filling their exquisitely-formed earthen jars, the dainty poise of their classic heads, and the flowing folds of their draperies have been actually present with her; and now?—why, it is like the entrance of a half-tipsy vagabond player bedizened in tawdry finery—the picture is blurred. She rests her head against the trunk of a pine tree behind her, and awaits the singer. She is sitting on an incline in the midst of a wilderness of trees; some have blown down, some have been cut down, and the lopped branches lie about; moss and bracken and trailing bramble, fir-cones, wild rose bushes, and speckled red 'fairy hats' fight for life in wild confusion. A disused quarry to the left is an ideal haunt of pike, and to the right a little river rushes along in haste to join a greater sister that is fighting a troubled way to the sea. A row of stepping-stones crosses it, and if you were to stand on one you would see shoals of restless stone loach 'Beardies' darting from side to side. The tails of several ducks can be seen above the water, and the paddle of their balancing feet, and the gurgling suction of their bills as they search for larvæ can be heard distinctly between the hum of insect, twitter of bird, and rustle of stream and leaf. The singer has changed his lay to a whistle, and presently he comes down the path a cool, neat, grey-clad figure, with a fishing creel slung across his back, and a trout rod held on his shoulder. The air ceases abruptly, and his cold grey eyes scan the seated figure with its gipsy ease of attitude, a scarlet shawl that has fallen from her shoulders forming an accentuative background to the slim roundness of her waist.

Persistent study, coupled with a varied experience of the female animal, has given the owner of the grey eyes some facility in classing her, although it has not supplied him with any definite data as to what any one of the species may do in a given circumstance. To put it in his own words, in answer to a friend who chaffed him on his untiring pursuit of women as an interesting problem :

'If a fellow has had much experience of his fellow-man he may divide him into types, and, given a certain number of men and a certain number of circumstances, he is pretty safe on hitting on the line of action each type will strike ; 't aint so with woman. You may always look out for the unexpected, she generally upsets a fellow's calculations, and you are never safe in laying odds on her. Tell you what, old chappie, we may talk about superior intellect; but, if a woman wasn't handicapped by her affection, or need of it, the cleverest chap in Christendom would be just a bit of putty in her hands. I find them more fascinating as problems than anything going. Never let an opportunity slip to get new data—never!'

He did not now. He met the frank, unembarrassed gaze of eyes that would have looked with just the same bright inquiry at the advent of a hare, or a toad, or any other object that might cross her path, and raised his hat with respectful courtesy, saying, in the drawling tone habitual with him—

'I hope I am not trespassing?'

'I can't say; you may be, so may I, but no one has ever told me so!'

A pause. His quick glance has noted the thick wedding ring on her slim brown hand, and the flash of a diamond in its keeper. A lady decidedly. Fast? perhaps. Original? undoubtedly. Worth knowing? rather.

'I am looking for a trout stream, but the

directions I got were rather vague; might I——'

'It's straight ahead, but you won't catch anything now, at least not here, sun's too glaring and water too low, a mile up you may, in an hour's time.'

'Oh, thanks awfully for the tip. You fish then?'

'Yes, sometimes.'

'Trout run big here?' (what odd eyes the woman has, kind of magnetic.)

'No, seldom over a pound, but they are very game.'

'Rare good sport isn't it, whipping a stream? There is so much besides the mere catching of fish. The river and the trees and the quiet sets a fellow thinking—kind of sermon—makes a chap feel good, don't it?'

She smiles assentingly. And yet what the devil is she amused at he queries mentally. An inspiration. He acts upon it, and says eagerly:

'I wonder—I don't half like to ask—but fishing puts people on a common footing, don't it? You knowing the stream, you know, would you tell me what are the best flies to use?'

'I tie my own, but——'

'Do you? how clever of you! wish I could,' and sitting down on the other end of the tree, he takes out his fly book, 'but I interrupted you, you were going to say?'

'Only,' stretching out her hand (of a perfect shape but decidedly brown) for the book, 'that you might give the local fly-tyer a trial, he'll tell you.'

'Later on, end of next month, or perhaps later, you might try the oak-fly, the natural fly you know; a horn is the best thing to hold them in, they get out of anything else—and put two on at a time.'

'By Jove, I must try that dodge!'

He watches her as she handles his book and examines the contents critically, turning aside some with a glance, fingering others almost tenderly, holding them daintily and noting the cock of wings and the hint of tinsel, with her head on one side; a trick of hers he thinks.

'Which do you like most, wet or dry fly?' (she is looking at some dry flies.)

'Oh,' with that rare smile, 'at the time I swear by whichever happens to catch most fish. Perhaps, really, dry fly. I fancy most of these flies are better for Scotland or England. Up to this March-brown has been the most killing thing. But you might try an "orange-grouse," that's always good here; with perhaps a "hare's ear" for a change—and put on a "coachman" for the evenings. My husband (he steals a side look at her) brought home some beauties yesterday evening.'

'Lucky fellow!'

She returns the book. There is a tone in his voice as he says this that jars on her, sensitive as she is to every inflection of a voice, with an intuition that is almost second sight. She gathers up her shawl. She has a cream-coloured woollen gown on, and her skin looks duskily foreign by contrast. She is on her feet before he can regain his, and says, with a cool little bend of her head: 'Good afternoon, I wish you a full basket!'

Before he can raise his cap she is down the slope, gliding with easy steps that have a strange grace, and then springing lightly from stone to stone across the stream. He feels small, snubbed someway, and he sits down on the spot where she sat and, lighting his pipe, says 'check!'

* * * * *

She is walking slowly up the garden path.

A man in his shirt sleeves is stooping amongst the tender young peas. A bundle of stakes lies next him, and he whistles softly and all out of tune as he twines the little tendrils round each new support. She looks at his broad shoulders and narrow flanks; his back is too long for great strength, she thinks. He hears her step, and smiles up at her from under the shadow of his broad-leafed hat.

'How do you feel now, old woman?'

'Beastly. I've got that horrid qualmish feeling again. I can't get rid of it.'

He has spread his coat on the side of the path and pats it for her to sit down.

'What is it' (anxiously)? 'if you were a mare I'd know what to do for you. Have a nip of whisky?'

He strides off without waiting for her reply and comes back with it and a biscuit, kneels down and holds the glass to her lips.

'Poor little woman, buck up! You'll see that'll fix you. Then you go by-and-by and have a shy at the fish.'

She is about to say something when a fresh qualm attacks her and she does not.

He goes back to his tying.

'By Jove!' he says suddenly, 'I forgot. Got something to show you!'

After a few minutes he returns carrying a basket covered with a piece of sacking. A dishevelled-looking hen, with spread wings trailing and her breast bare from sitting on her eggs, screeches after him. He puts it carefully down and uncovers it, disclosing seven little balls of yellow fluff splashed with olive green. They look up sideways with bright round eyes, and their little spoon bills look disproportionately large.

'Aren't they beauties (enthusiastically)? This one is just out,' taking up an egg, 'mustn't let it get chilled.' There is a chip out of it and a piece of hanging skin. 'Isn't it funny?' he asks, showing her how it is curled in the shell, with its paddles flattened and its bill breaking through the chip, and the slimy feathers sticking to its violet skin.

She suppresses an exclamation of disgust, and looks at his fresh-tinted skin instead. He is covering basket, hen, and all—

'How you love young things!' she says.

'Some. I had a filly once, she turned out a lovely mare! I cried when I had to sell her, I wouldn't have let any one in God's world mount her.'

'Yes, you would!'

'Who?' with a quick look of resentment.

'Me!'

'I wouldn't!'

'What! you wouldn't?'

'I wouldn't!'

'I think you would if I wanted to!' with a flash out of the tail of her eye.

'No, I wouldn't!'

'Then you would care more for her than for me. I would give you your choice (passionately), her or me!'

'What nonsense!'

'May be (concentrated), but it's lucky she isn't here to make deadly sense of it.' A humble-bee buzzes close to her ear, and she is roused to a sense of facts, and laughs to think how nearly they have quarrelled over a mare that was sold before she knew him.

* * * *

Some evenings later, she is stretched motionless in a chair, and yet she conveys an impression of restlessness; a sensitively nervous person would feel it. She is gazing at her husband, her brows are drawn together, and make three little lines. He is reading, reading quietly, without moving his eyes quickly from side to side of the page as she does when she reads, and he pulls away at a big pipe with steady enjoyment. Her eyes turn from him to the window, and follow the course of two clouds, then they close for a few seconds, then open to watch him again. He looks up and smiles.

'Finished your book?'

There is a singular soft monotony in his voice; the organ with which she replies is capable of more varied expression.

'Yes, it is a book makes one think. It would be a greater book if he were not an Englishman. He's afraid of shocking the big middle class. You wouldn't care about it.'

'Finished your smoke?'

'No, it went out, too much fag to light up again! No (protestingly), never you mind, old boy, why do you?'

He has drawn his long length out of his chair, and, kneeling down beside her, guards a lighted match from the incoming evening air. She draws in the smoke contentedly, and her eyes smile back with a general vague tenderness.

'Thank you, dear old man!'

'Going out again?' negative head shake.

'Back aching?' affirmative nod, accompanied by a steadily aimed puff of smoke, that she has been carefully inhaling, into his eyes.

'Scamp! Have your booties off?'

'Oh, don't you bother, Lizzie will do it!'

He has seized a foot from under the rocker, and, sitting on his heels, holds it on his knee, whilst he unlaces the boot; then he loosens the stocking under her toes, and strokes her foot gently.

'Now, the other!' Then he drops both boots outside the door, and fetching a little pair of slippers, past their first smartness, from the bedroom, puts one on. He examines the left foot; it is a little swollen round the ankle, and he presses his broad fingers gently round it as one sees a man do to a horse with windgalls. Then he pulls the rocker nearer to his chair and rests the slipperless foot on his thigh. He relights his pipe, takes up his book, and rubs softly from ankle to toes as he reads.

She smokes and watches him, diverting herself by imagining him in the hats of different periods. His is a delicate-skinned face with regular features; the eyes are fine, in colour and shape with the luminous clearness of a child's; his pointed beard is soft and curly. She looks at his hand,—a broad strong hand with capable fingers,—the hand of a craftsman, a contradiction to the face with its distinguished delicacy. She holds her own up with a cigarette poised between the first and second fingers, idly pleased with its beauty of form and delicate nervous slightness. One speculation chases the other in her quick brain; odd questions as to race arise; she dives into theories as to the why and wherefore of their distinctive natures, and holds a mental debate in which she takes both sides of the question impartially. He has finished his pipe, laid down his book, and is gazing dreamily, with his eyes darkened by their long lashes, and a look of tender melancholy in their clear depths, into space.

'What are you thinking of?' There is a look of expectation in her quivering nervous little face.

He turns to her, chafing her ankle again.

'I was wondering if lob-worms would do for——'

He stops. A strange look of disappointment

flits across her face and is lost in an hysterical peal of laughter.

'You are the best emotional check I ever knew,' she gasps.

He stares at her in utter bewilderment, and then a slow smile creeps to his eyes and curves the thin lips under his moustache, a smile at her.

'You seem amused, Gipsy!'

She springs out of her chair and seizes book and pipe; he follows the latter anxiously with his eyes until he sees it laid safely on the table. Then she perches herself, resting her knees against one of his legs, whilst she hooks her feet back under the other—

'Now I am all up, don't I look small?'

He smiles his slow smile. 'Yes, I believe you are made of gutta percha.'

She is stroking out all the lines in his face with the tip of her finger; then she runs it through his hair. He twists his head half impatiently, she desists.

'I divide all the people in the world,' she says, 'into those who like their hair played with, and those who don't. Having my hair brushed gives me more pleasure than anything else; it's delicious. I'd *purr* if I knew how. I notice (meditatively) I am never in sympathy with those who don't like it; I am with those who do. I always get on with them.'

'You are a queer little devil!'

'Am I? I shouldn't have thought you would have found out I was the latter at all. I wish I were a man! I believe if I were a man, I'd be a disgrace to my family.'

'Why?'

'I'd go on a jolly old spree!'

He laughs: 'Poor little woman, is it so dull?'

There is a gleam of devilry in her eyes, and she whispers solemnly—

'Begin with a D,' and she traces imaginary letters across his forehead, and ending with a flick over his ear, says, 'and that is the tail of the y!'

After a short silence she queries—

'Are you fond of me?' She is rubbing her chin up and down his face.

'Of course I am, don't you know it?'

'Yes, perhaps I do,' impatiently; 'but I want to be told it. A woman doesn't care a fig for a love as deep as the death-sea and as silent, she wants something that tells her it in little waves all the time. It isn't the love, you know, it 's the being loved; it isn't really the man, it 's his loving!'

'By Jove, you 're a rum un!'

'I wish I wasn't then. I wish I was as commonplace as——. You don't tell me anything about myself (a fierce little kiss), you might, even if it were lies. Other men who cared for me told me things about my eyes, my hands, anything. I don't believe you notice.'

'Yes I *do*, little one, only I think it.'

'Yes, but I don't care a bit for your thinking; if I can't see what 's in your head what good is it to me?'

'I wish I could understand you, dear!'

'I wish to God you could. Perhaps if you were badder and I were gooder we 'd meet half-way. *You* are an awfully good old chap; it 's just men like you send women like me to the devil!'

'But you are good (kissing her), a real good chum! You understand a fellow's weak points. You don't blow him up if he gets on a bit. Why (enthusiastically), being married to you is like chumming with a chap! Why (admiringly), do you remember before we were married, when I let that card fall out of my pocket? Why, I couldn't have told another girl about her. She wouldn't have believed that I *was* straight. She'd have thrown me over. And you sent her a quid because she was sick. You are a great little woman!'

'Don't see it! (she is biting his ear). Perhaps I was a man last time, and some hereditary memories are cropping up in this incarnation!'

He looks so utterly at sea that she has to laugh again, and, kneeling up, shuts his eyes with kisses, and bites his chin and shakes it like a terrier in her strong little teeth.

'You imp! was there ever such a woman!'

Catching her wrists, he parts his knees and drops her on to the rug. Then, perhaps the subtle magnetism that is in her affects him, for he stoops and snatches her up and carries her up and down, and then over to the window and lets the fading light with its glimmer of moonshine play on her odd face with its tantalising changes. His eyes dilate and his colour deepens as he crushes her soft little body to him and carries her off to her room.

* * * * *

Summer is waning and the harvest is ripe for ingathering, and the voice of the reaping machine is loud in the land. She is stretched on her back on the short heather-mixed moss at the side of a bog stream. Rod and creel are flung aside, and the wanton breeze, with the breath of coolness it has gathered in its passage over the murky dykes of black bog water, is playing with the tail fly, tossing it to and fro with a half threat to fasten it to a prickly spine of golden gorse. Bunches of bog-wool nod their fluffy heads, and through the myriad indefinite sounds comes the regular scrape of a strickle on the scythe of a reaper in a neighbouring meadow. Overhead a flotilla of clouds is steering from the south in a north-easterly direction. Her eyes follow them. Old time galleons, she thinks, with their wealth of snowy sail spread, riding breast to breast up a wide blue fjord after victory. The sails of the last are rose flushed, with a silver edge. Somehow she thinks of Cleopatra sailing down to meet Antony, and a great longing fills her soul to sail off somewhere too—away from the daily need of dinner-getting and the recurring Monday with its washing; life with its tame duties and virtuous monotony. She fancies herself in Arabia on the back of a swift steed. Flashing eyes set in dark faces surround her, and she can see the clouds of sand swirl, and feel the swing under her of his rushing stride. Her thoughts shape themselves into a wild song, a song to her steed of flowing mane and satin skin; an uncouth rhythmical jingle with a feverish beat; a song to the untamed spirit that dwells in her. Then she fancies she is on the stage of an ancient theatre out in the open air, with hundreds of faces upturned towards her. She is gauze-clad in a cobweb garment of wondrous tissue. Her arms are clasped by jewelled snakes, and one with quivering diamond fangs coils round her hips. Her hair floats loosely, and her feet are sandal-clad, and the delicate breath of vines and the salt freshness of an incoming sea seems to fill her nostrils. She bounds forward and dances, bends her lissom waist, and curves her slender arms, and gives to the soul of each man what he craves, be it good or evil. And she can feel now, lying here in the shade of

Irish hills with her head resting on her scarlet shawl and her eyes closed, the grand intoxicating power of swaying all these human souls to wonder and applause. She can see herself with parted lips and panting, rounded breasts, and a dancing devil in each glowing eye, sway voluptuously to the wild music that rises, now slow, now fast, now deliriously wild, seductive, intoxicating, with a human note of passion in its strain. She can feel the answering shiver of feeling that quivers up to her from the dense audience, spellbound by the motion of her glancing feet, and she flies swifter and swifter, and lighter and lighter, till the very serpents seem alive with jewelled scintillations. One quivering, gleaming, daring bound, and she stands with outstretched arms and passion-filled eyes, poised on one slender foot, asking a supreme note to finish her dream of motion. And the men rise to a man and answer her, and cheer, cheer till the echoes shout from the surrounding hills and tumble wildly down the crags. The clouds have sailed away, leaving long feathery streaks in their wake. Her eyes have an inseeing look, and she is tremulous with excitement. She can hear yet that last grand shout, and the strain of that old-time music that she has never heard in this life of hers, save as an inner accompaniment to the memory of hidden things, born with her, not of this time.

And her thoughts go to other women she has known, women good and bad, school friends, casual acquaintances, women workers—joyless machines for grinding daily corn, unwilling maids grown old in the endeavour to get settled, patient wives who bear little ones to indifferent husbands until they wear out—a long array. She busies herself with questioning. Have they, too, this thirst for excitement, for change, this restless craving for sun and love and motion? Stray words, half confidences, glimpses through soul-chinks of suppressed fires, actual outbreaks, domestic catastrophes, how the ghosts dance in the cells of her memory! And she laughs, laughs softly to herself because the denseness of man, his chivalrous conservative devotion to the female idea he has created blinds him, perhaps happily, to the problems of her complex nature. Ay, she mutters musingly, the wisest of them can only say we are enigmas. Each one of them sets about solving the riddle of the *ewig weibliche*

—and well it is that the workings of our hearts are closed to them, that we are cunning enough or *great* enough to seem to be what they would have us, rather than be what we are. But few of them have had the insight to find out the key to our seeming contradictions. The why a refined, physically fragile woman will mate with a brute, a mere male animal with primitive passions—and love him—the why strength and beauty appeal more often than the more subtly fine qualities of mind or heart —the why women (and not the innocent ones) will condone sins that men find hard to forgive in their fellows. They have all overlooked the eternal wildness, the untamed primitive savage temperament that lurks in the mildest, best woman. Deep in through ages of convention this primeval trait burns, an untameable quantity that may be concealed but is never eradicated by culture — the keynote of woman's witchcraft and woman's strength. But it is there, sure enough, and each woman is conscious of it in her truth-telling hours of quiet self-scrutiny—and each woman in God's wide world will deny it, and each woman will help another to conceal it—for the woman who tells the truth and is not a liar about these things is untrue to her sex and abhorrent to man, for he has fashioned a model on imaginary lines, and he has said, 'so I would have you,' and every woman is an unconscious liar, for so man loves her. And when a Strindberg or a Nietzche arises and peers into the recesses of her nature and dissects her ruthlessly, the men shriek out louder than the women, because the truth is at all times unpalatable, and the gods they have set up are dear to them. . . .'

'Dreaming, or speering into futurity? You have the look of a seer. I believe you are half a witch!'

And he drops his grey-clad figure on the turf. He has dropped his drawl long ago, in midsummer.

'Is not every woman that? Let us hope I 'm, for my friends, a white one.'

'A-ah! Have you many friends?'

'That is a query! If you mean many correspondents, many persons who send me Christmas cards, or remember my birthday, or figure in my address-book? No.'

'Well, grant I don't mean that!'

'Well, perhaps, yes. Scattered over the

world, if my death were belled out, many women would give me a tear, and some a prayer. And many men would turn back a page in their memory and give me a kind thought, perhaps a regret, and go back to their work with a feeling of having lost something—that they never possessed. I am a creature of moments. Women have told me that I came into their lives just when they needed me. Men had no need to tell me, I felt it. People have needed me more than I them. I have given freely whatever they craved from me in the way of understanding or love. I have touched sore places they showed me and healed them, but they never got at me. I have been for myself, and helped myself, and borne the burden of my own mistakes. Some have chafed at my self-sufficiency and have called me fickle—not understanding that they gave me nothing, and that when I had served them, their moment was ended, and I was to pass on. I read people easily, I am written in black letter to most——'

'To your husband!'

'He (quickly)—we will not speak of him; it is not loyal.'

'Do not I understand you a little?'

'You do not misunderstand me.'

'That is something.'

'It is much!'

'Is it? (searching her face). It is not one grain of sand in the desert that stretches between you and me, and you are as impenetrable as a sphinx at the end of it. This (passionately) is my moment, and what have you given me?'

'Perhaps less than other men I have known; but you want less. You are a little like me, you can stand alone. And yet (her voice is shaking), have I given you nothing?'

He laughs, and she winces—and they sit silent, and they both feel as if the earth between them is laid with infinitesimal electric threads vibrating with a common pain. Her eyes are filled with tears that burn but don't fall, and she can see his somehow through her closed lids, see their cool greyness troubled by sudden fire, and she rolls her handkerchief into a moist cambric ball between her cold palms.

'You have given me something—something to carry away with me—an infernal want. You ought to be satisfied. I am infernally miserable.'

'You (nearer) have the most tantalising mouth in the world when your lips tremble like that. I . . . What! can you cry? You?'

'Yes, even I can cry!'

'You dear woman! (pause) And I can't help you!'

'You can't help me. No man can. Don't think it is because you are you I cry, but because you probe a little nearer into the real me that I feel so.'

'Was it necessary to say that? (reproachfully). Do you think I don't know it? I can't for the life of me think how you, with that free gipsy nature of yours, could bind yourself to a monotonous country life, with no excitement, no change. I wish I could offer you my yacht. Do you like the sea?'

'I love it, it answers one's moods.'

'Well, let us play pretending, as the children say. Grant that I could, I would hang your cabin with your own colours; fill it with books, all those I have heard you say you care for; make it a nest as rare as the bird it would shelter. You would reign supreme; when your highness would deign to honour her servant I would come and humour your every whim. If you were glad, you could clap your hands and order music, and we would dance on the white deck, and we would skim through the sunshine of Southern seas on a spice-scented breeze. You make me poetical. And if you were angry you could vent your feelings on me, and I would give in and bow my head to your mood. And we would drop anchor and stroll through strange cities, go far inland and glean folk-lore out of the beaten track of everyday tourists. And at night when the harbour slept we would sail out through the moonlight over silver seas. You are smiling, you look so different when you smile; do you like my picture?'

'Some of it!'

'What not?'

'You!'

'Thank you.'

'You asked me. Can't you understand where the spell lies? It is the freedom, the freshness, the vague danger, the unknown that has a witchery for me, ay, for every woman!'

'Are you incapable of affection, then?'

'Of course not, I share' (bitterly) 'that crowning disability of my sex. But not willingly, I chafe under it. My God, if it were not for that, we women would master the world. I tell you men would be no match for us. At heart we care nothing for laws, nothing for systems. All your elaborately reasoned codes for controlling morals or man do not weigh a jot with us against an impulse, an instinct. We learn those things from you, you tamed, amenable animals; they are not natural to us. It is a wise disposition of providence that this untameableness of ours is corrected by our affections. We forge our own chains in a moment of softness, and then' (bitterly) 'we may as well wear them with a good grace. Perhaps many of our seeming contradictions are only the outward evidences of inward chafing. Bah! the qualities that go to make a Napoleon—superstition, want of honour, disregard of opinion and the eternal I—are oftener to be found in a woman than a man. Lucky for the world perhaps that all these attributes weigh as nothing in the balance with the need to love if she be a good woman, to be loved if she is of a coarser fibre.'

'I never met any one like you, you are a strange woman!'

'No, I am merely a truthful one. Women talk to me—why, I can't say—but always they come, strip their hearts and souls naked, and let me see the hidden folds of their natures. The greatest tragedies I have ever read are child's play to those I have seen acted in the inner life of outwardly commonplace women. A woman must beware of speaking the truth to a man; he loves her the less for it. It is the elusive spirit in her that he divines but cannot seize, that fascinates and keeps him.'

There is a long silence, the sun is waning and the scythes are silent, and overhead the crows are circling, a croaking irregular army, homeward bound from a long day's pillage.

She has made no sign, yet so subtly is the air charged with her that he feels but a few moments remain to him. He goes over and kneels beside her and fixes his eyes on her odd dark face. They both tremble, yet neither speaks. His breath is coming quickly, and the bistre stains about her eyes seem to have deepened, perhaps by contrast as she has paled.

'Look at me!'

She turns her head right round and gazes straight into his face. A few drops of sweat glisten on his forehead.

'You witch woman! what am I to do with myself? Is my moment ended?'

'I think so.'

'Lord, what a mouth!'

'Don't, oh don't!'

'No, I won't. But do you mean it? Am I, who understand your every mood, your restless spirit, to vanish out of your life? You can't mean it. Listen; are you listening to me? I can't see your face; take down your hands. Go back over every chance meeting you and I have had together since I met you first by the river, and judge them fairly. To-day is Monday; Wednesday afternoon I shall pass your gate, and if—if my moment is ended, and you mean to send me away, to let me go with this weary aching . . .'

'A-ah!' she stretches out one brown hand appealingly, but he does not touch it.

'*Hang something white on the lilac bush!*'

She gathers up creel and rod, and he takes her shawl, and, wrapping it round her, holds her a moment in it, and looks searchingly into her eyes, then stands back and raises his hat, and she glides away through the reedy grass.

* * * * *

Wednesday morning she lies watching the clouds sail by. A late rose spray nods into the open window, and the petals fall every time. A big bee buzzes in and fills the room with his bass note, and then dances out again. She can hear his footstep on the gravel. Presently he looks in over the half window.

'Get up and come out, 'twill do you good. Have a brisk walk!'

She shakes her head languidly, and he throws a great soft dewy rose with sure aim on her breast.

'Shall I go in and lift you out and put you, "nighty" and all, into your tub?'

'No (impatiently). I 'll get up just now.'

The head disappears, and she rises wearily and gets through her dressing slowly, stopped every moment by a feeling of faintness. He finds her presently rocking slowly to and fro with closed eyes, and drops a leaf with three plums in it on to her lap.

'I have been watching four for the last week, but a bird, greedy beggar, got one this morning early—try them. Don't you mind, old girl, I 'll pour out my own tea!'

She bites into one and tries to finish it, but cannot.

'You are a good old man!' she says, and the tears come unbidden to her eyes, and trickle down her cheeks, dropping on to the plums, streaking their delicate bloom. He looks uneasily at her, but doesn't know what to do, and when he has finished his breakfast he stoops over her chair and strokes her hair, saying, as he leaves a kiss on the top of her head—

'Come out into the air, little woman; do you a world of good!' And presently she hears the sharp thrust of his spade above the bee's hum, leaf rustle, and the myriad late summer sounds that thrill through the air. It irritates her almost to screaming point. There is a practical non-sympathy about it, she can distinguish the regular one, two, three, the thrust, interval, then pat, pat, on the upturned sod. To-day she wants some one, and her thoughts wander to the grey-eyed man who never misunderstands her, and she wonders what he would say to her. Oh, she wants some one so badly to soothe her. And she yearns for the little mother who is twenty years under the daisies. The little mother who is a faint memory strengthened by a daguerreotype in which she sits with silkmittened hands primly crossed on the lap of her moiré gown, a diamond brooch fastening the black velvet ribbon crossed so stiffly over her lace collar, the shining tender eyes looking steadily out, and her hair in the fashion of fifty-six. How that spade dominates over every sound! And what a sickening pain she has; an odd pain, she never felt it before. Supposing she were to die, she tries to fancy how she would look. They would be sure to plaster her curls down. He might be digging her grave—no, it is the patch where the early peas grew; the peas that were eaten with the twelve weeks' ducklings; she remembers them, little fluffy golden balls with waxen bills, and such dainty paddles. Remembers holding an egg to her ear and listening to it cheep inside before even there was a chip in the shell. Strange how things come to life. What! she sits bolt upright and holds tightly to the chair, and a questioning, awesome look comes over her face. Then the quick blood creeps up through her olive skin right up to her temples, and she buries her face in her hands and sits so a long time.

The maid comes in and watches her curiously,

and moves softly about. The look in her eyes is the look of a faithful dog, and she loves her with the same rare fidelity. She hesitates, then goes into the bedroom and stands thoughtfully, with her hands clasped over her breast.

She is a tall, thin, flat-waisted woman, with misty blue eyes and a receding chin. Her hair is pretty.

She turns as her mistress comes in, with an expectant look on her face. She has taken up a night-gown, but holds it idly.

'Lizzie, had you ever a child?'

The girl's long left hand is ringless, yet she asks it with a quiet insistence as if she knew what the answer would be, and the odd eyes read her face with an almost cruel steadiness. The girl flushes painfully and then whitens, her very eyes seem to pale, and her under lip twitches as she jerks out huskily—

'Yes!'

'What happened it?'

'It died, Ma'm.'

'Poor thing! Poor old Liz!'

She pats the girl's hand softly, and the latter stands dumbly and looks down at both hands, as if fearful to break the wonder of a caress. She whispers hesitatingly—

'Have you, have you any little things left?'

And she laughs such a soft, cooing little laugh, like the churring of a ring-dove, and nods shyly back in reply to the tall maid's questioning look. The latter goes out, and comes back with a flat, red-painted deal box and unlocks it. It does not hold very much, and the tiny garments are not of costly material, but the two women pore over them as a gem collector over a rare stone. She has a glimpse of thick crested paper as the girl unties a packet of letters, and looks away until she says tenderly—

'Look, Ma'm!'

A little bit of hair inside a paper heart. It is almost white, so silky, and so fine, that it is more like a thread of bog wool than a baby's hair. And the mistress, who is a wife, puts her arms round the tall maid, who has never had more than a moral claim to the name, and kisses her in her quick way.

The afternoon is drawing on; she is kneeling before an open trunk with flushed cheeks and sparkling eyes. A heap of unused, dainty lace trimmed ribbon-decked cambric garments is scattered around her. She holds the soft scented web to her cheek and smiles musingly. Then she rouses herself and sets to work, sorting out the finest, with the narrowest lace and tiniest ribbon, and puckers her swarthy brows, and measures lengths along her middle finger. Then she gets slowly up, as if careful of herself as a precious thing, and half afraid.

'Lizzie!'

'Yes, Ma'm!'

'Wasn't it lucky they were too fine for every day? They will be so pretty. Look at this one with the tiny valenciennes edging. Why, one nightgown will make a dozen little shirts—such elfin-shirts as they are too—and Lizzie!'

'Yes, Ma'm!'

'Just hang it out on the lilac bush; mind, the lilac bush!'

'Yes, Ma'm.'

'Or Lizzie, wait—I'll do it myself!'

NOW SPRING HAS COME

A CONFIDENCE

'When the spring time comes, gentle Annie, and the flowers are blossoming on the plain!
Lal, lal, la, la, la, lallallalla, lal, lal, lal, la, la, la, la, la,
When the spring time comes, gentle Annie, and the mockin' bird is singing on the tree!' . . .

'I DON'T believe that mocking-bird line belongs to the song at all, Lizzie, you never do get a thing right!'

The words have a partly irritated, partly contemptuous tone that seems oddly at variance with the size of the child who utters them. She is lying flat on her stomach on the floor, resting her elbows at each side of a book she is reading, holding her sharp chin in the palms of her hands, waving her skinny legs in unconscious time to the half tired, half feverish lilt of the nurse as she jogs the baby in time to the tune. She gazes, as she speaks, at the girl with a pair of unusually bright penetrating eyes. This mocking-bird line never fails to annoy her.

'Troth, an if I cud get the young limb to slape I wouldn't care if 'twas mockin'-birds or tom-cats!' is the indifferent answer.

* * * * * *

Strange how some trivial thing will jog a link in a chain of association, and set it vibrating until it brings one face to face with scenes and people long forgotten in some prison cell in one's brain; calling to new life a red-haired girl, with sherry-brown eyes, and a flat back, pacing a nursery floor in impatient endeavour to get a fractious child to sleep—ay, her very voice and her persistent mixing of mocking-birds and spring time. So muses the child twenty years after, as, past her first youth, with only the eyes and the smile unchanged, she lies on a bear-skin before the fire on a chilly evening in late spring, and goes over a recent experience. A half humorous smile with a tinge of mockery in it plays round her lips as she says—

'Twenty years ago. Queer how it should fit in after all that time!'

* * * * * *

'Tell you how it was? That is not very easy, pathos may become bathos in the telling. Let me see. Of course it was chance, or is there any such thing as chance? Say fate, instead. The three old ladies who spin our destinies were in want of amusement, so they pitched on me. They sent their messenger to me in the guise of a paper-backed novel with a taking name. I was waiting in a shop for some papers I had ordered when it struck me. I took it up. The author was unknown to me. I opened it at haphazard and a line caught me. I read on. I was roused by the bookseller's suave voice.

'That is a very bad book, Madam. One of the modern realistic school, a *tendenz roman*, I would not advise Madam to read it!'

'A-ah, indeed!'

I laid it down and left the shop, but the words I had read kept dancing before me, I saw them written across the blue of the sky, in the sun streaks on the pavement, and the luminous delicacy of the Norwegian summer nights. They were impressed on my brain in vivid colour, glowing, blushing with ardour as they were. Weeks passed; one afternoon time hung heavily on my hands, and I sent for the book. I read all that afternoon; let the telling words, the passionate pain, the hungry yearning, all the tragedy of a man's soul-strife with evil and destiny, sorrow and sin, bite into my sentient being. When the book was finished I was consumed with a desire to see and know the author. I never reasoned that the whole struggle might only be an extraordinarily clever intuitive analysis of a possible experience. I accepted it as real, and I wanted to help this man. I longed to tell him in his loneness, that one human being, and that one a woman, had courage to help him. The abstract ego of the novel haunted me. I have a will of my own, so I set to work to find him. It was not so easy. None of my acquaintances knew him, or of him. He was a strange meteor, and as the book was condemned by the orthodox I had to feel my way cautiously. Isn't it dreadful to think what slaves we are to custom? I wonder shall we ever be able to tell the truth, ever be able to live fearlessly according to our own light, to believe that what is right for us must be right? It seems as if all the religions, all the advancement, all the culture of the past, has only been a forging of chains to cripple posterity, a laborious building up of moral and legal prisons based on false conceptions of sin and shame, to cramp men's minds and hearts and souls, not to speak of women's. What half creatures we are, we women! Hermaphrodite by force of circumstances. Deformed results of a fight of centuries between physical suppression and natural impulse to fulfil our destiny. Every social revolution has told hardest on us: when a sacrifice was demanded, let woman make it. And yet there are men, and the best of them, who see all this and would effect a change, if they knew how. Why it came about? Because men manufactured an artificial morality, made sins of things that were as clean in themselves as the pairing of birds on the wing; crushed nature, robbed it of its beauty and meaning, and established a system that means war, and always war, because it is a struggle between instinctive truths and cultivated lies. Yes, I know I speak hotly, but my heart burns in me sometimes, and I hate myself. It's a bad thing when a man or woman has a contempt for himself. There's nothing like a good dose of love fever (in other words, a waking to the fact that one is a higher animal with a destiny to fulfil) to teach one self-knowledge, to give one a glimpse into the contradictory issues of one's individual nature. Study yourself, and what will you find? Just what I did; the weak, the inconsequent, the irresponsible. In one word, the untrue feminine is of man's making, whilst the strong, the natural, the true womanly is of God's making. It is easy to read as a primer; but how change it? Go back to my poet! Well, at length an old bookseller I knew gave me surer information. My intuition was not at fault, the experiences were wrung from the man's soul. As the old superstition has it, a dagger dipped in a man's heart-blood will always strike home, so no wonder they pierced me with their passion, despair, and brave endurance. What the old fellow wrote to him I know not, but I got an unconventional pretty letter from him, and it ended in our writing to one another.

As my time to leave drew near, the desire to see him became overpowering. I could afford it; he could not. It ended in our arranging to meet at a little town on the coast. It is strange how the idea of a person one has never seen can possess one as completely as this did me. I, who, as you know, think as little of starting alone for say, Mexico, as another woman of going to afternoon tea, who have trotted the globe without male assistance, felt as tremulously stirred as at confirmation day. There are days that stand out in the gallery of one's remembrances clean painted as a Van de Hooge, with a sharp clearness. I slept on board, and early the next morning, it was Sunday, I stood on deck watching the coast as we glided through the water that danced in delicious September sunshine. I was happily expectant. At dinner hour we passed a fjord, a lovely deep blue fjord winding to our right as we passed, with the spire of a church just visible amongst the fir trees round the bend. Boats of all kinds, from a smart cutter to a pram were coming out after the service. The white sails swelled as they caught the breeze, flapped as they tacked, hung listlessly a second, and then dashed with a swerve, like swift snowy-winged birds, through the water. I had not troubled with church-going of late years. Why? oh, speculation—weariness of soul that found no drop of consolation in religious observance, maybe that might be the reason. But all those honest simple folks in their Sunday bravery, fair-haired girls with their psalm-books wrapped up in their only silk kerchief, the ring of laughter echoing across the water, the magic of sun and sky, mountain and fjord, made me feel that I, too, was church-going, and I felt strangely happy. It is the off-moments that we do not count as playing any part in our lives that are, after all, the best we have. I am afraid it would be impossible to make you see things as I felt them. I went up to the hotel when I landed; I had the reputation of riches, the hotel was at my service. I inquire for him, go down to my sitting-room, send him my card, and wait. I wait with an odd feeling that I am outside myself, watching myself as it were. I can see the very childishness of my figure, the too slight hips and bust, the flash of rings on my fingers; they are pressed against my heart, for it is beating hatefully; ay, the very expectant side-poise of head is visible to me somehow. It flashes across me as I stand that so might a slave wait for the coming of a new master, and I laugh at myself for my want-wit agitation. A knock. . . . 'Come in!' . . . The door opens, and I am satisfied. In the space of a second's gaze I meet what my soul has been waiting for,—ah, how long? I think always: Have I lived before in some other life, that no surprise touches me? That it is just as if I am only meeting the embodiment of a disintegrated floating image that has often flashed before my consciousness, and flown before I could fix it? Has this man or some psychical part of this man been in touch with me before, or how is it? I stand still and stretch out my hand. I check an impulse to put out both. I feel so tremulously happy. I know before he speaks how his voice will sound, what his touch will be like before he clasps my hand. It is odd how the most important crisis of our lives often comes upon us in the most commonplace way. It is the fashion to decry love, yet the vehemence of the denials, the keenness of the weapons of satire and scepticism that are turned against it, only prove its existence. As long as man is man and woman is woman, it will be to them at some time the sweetest, and possibly the most fatal interest in life. Thrust it aside for ambition or gain, slight it as you will, sooner or later it will have its revenge. I had felt no breath of it as maid, wife, or widow, my heart had been a free, wild, shy thing, jessed by my will. Sometimes, by way of experiment, I let it fly to some one for an hour, but always to call it back again to my own safe keeping. Now it left me. We sat and talked, rather I talked, I think, and he listened. He said my going to see him even on literary grounds was eccentric, but then it seemed I had a way of doing as I pleased without exciting much comment. How did he know that? Oh, he had heard it! Was I really going away? How tiresome it was, really awfully tiresome! What was he like? Well, an American bison or a lion. You might put his head amongst the rarest and handsomest heads in the world. Prejudiced in his favour! No, not a bit. His hands, for instance, are great labourer's hands, freckled too; I don't like his gait either, indeed a dozen things. What we talked about? well, as I said, he listened mostly, laughed with a great joyous boyish laugh with a deep musical note in it. He has a deferential manner and a very caressing smile; a trick, too, of throwing back his head and tossing his crest of hair. Why he laughed? well, I suppose I made him. I told him all about myself, turned myself inside out, good and bad alike, as one might the pocket of an old gown, laughed at my own expense, hid nothing. An extraordinary thing to do, was it? I suppose it was—but the whole thing was rather unusual. He got up and walked about. Sometimes he thrust his hands in his pockets and exclaimed 'The Deuce,' etc. I fancy he learnt a good deal about me in a few hours. You see it was not as if one were talking to a stranger, it was as if one had met part of one's self one had lost for a long time and was filling up the gaps made during the absence. You can't understand. I think we were both very happy. He admired—no, that is not the word—he was taken with me, that is better. He said my hands were 'as small as a child's,' the tablecloth was dark red plush that made a good background. He pointed timidly, as a great shy boy might, to one of my rings. You see they don't as a rule wear many rings up there. I suppose they gave an impression of wealth. 'That one is very beautiful!' I laughed, I was so glad my hands were pretty; pretty hands last so much longer than a pretty face. I laughed too at his finger, it had such a deferential expression about it, and I called him a great child. I think we were both like two great children, we had found a common interest to rejoice in—we had found ourselves.

Every moment was delightful, we were making discoveries, finding we had had like experiences, had both hungered, both known want, were both of an age. We were both unconventional, and were shaking hands mentally all the time. I don't remember now what it was he said, but I remember I was obliged to drop my head, and I felt I was smiling from sheer delicious pleasure. He cried laughingly: 'You say I am a great child, you are a child yourself when you smile!' He was to have supper with me, and he went away for an hour. After he left I walked over to a long mirror and looked at myself. Tried to fancy how *he* saw me; that might be different, you know. I had colour, life, eyes like stars, trembling, smiling lips. There was something quivering, alert about me. I scarce knew myself. Of course the same hips, figure, features were reflected there—it was something shining through that struck me as foreign. Do you know what I did? I danced all round the room. Shows what an idiot an old woman can be. By the way, he denied that I was old. I was like a little girl—but a remarkable little girl. No wonder people always noticed me, as if I were a somebody. How did he know that? oh, he had heard it, for that matter seen it too, at the pier. He knew the moment I stepped off the boat that it was I. Yes, people always stared at me, but how could he know? Ah! presentiment perhaps. So he was on the pier? why did he not come and meet me? No audible answer, but a slow reddening up to the roots of his fair hair. I do not know quite how he conveyed it, but I had the sensation, a charming one, of being treated as a queen. But to go back. I sat or rather lay in an arm-chair at the window and watched the water and the ships. It was getting dusk, the luminous dusk of the north, as if a soft transparent purple veil is being dropped gently over the world. The fjord was full of lights from the different crafts at anchor, and the heaven full of stars, and the longer one looked up there, the more one saw myriads of glimmering eyes of light, until one's brain seemed full of their brightness, and one forgot one's body in gazing. Long silvery streaks glistened through the heaving water, like the flash of feeding trout, and lads and lasses in boats rowed to and fro, and human vibration seemed to thrill from them, filling the atmosphere with man and woman. And the silken air caressed my face as the touch of cool soft fingers. I had a feeling of perfect well-being; one does not get many such moments in one's life, does one? I think I just was happy, rehearsing the hours that flew too quickly, recalling every look, tone, gesture, and smile. The *jomfru* came in to lay the table. She knew me from a previous visit and began to talk, but I wanted to be alone with my thoughts. So I went up stairs, washed my hands and puffed them with sweet-smelling powder, and then when I went down again and sat and waited, I clasped them up over my head to make them white. He came back, flung his hat on the sofa out of sheer boyish delight at being back, came over and stood and looked down at me and I laughed up to him. If I were to talk until Doomsday, I could not make you understand what I cannot yet understand myself. After supper, at which I just sipped my tea and watched him, we sat at the window and looked out at the purple world. I had told him he might smoke. . . Well? well, we talked, and we talked when we were both silent, and he, I mean his thinking self came to me, and I, well, I believe, from the moment he came into the room, all the best of me went straight to him. The lights out in the harbour twinkled, a star fell, and I wished—well, wishes are foolish. I think he must have been watching my face, for when our eyes met, he smiled as if he understood. Sometimes he jumped up and stood rocking a chair backwards and forwards. He was sorry I was going away! Yes? oh, we might meet again! That might be difficult! Indeed? I should have thought *he* would be the last person in the world to say it was difficult to meet. He laughed at that, with a quick sidelong look he has, like a Finn dog; and said I was sharp, awfully sharp, as if he liked being caught. By the way, he occasionally used strong language, said I must forgive him, he wasn't very used to ladies' society.

At ten I said I would say good-night for conventionality's sake. He begged, humbly it struck me, for a little longer. I was to leave by the steamer at eight in the morning—would be down at seven—he might come to me. Would I give him a portrait of myself? Yes, I would get one specially done. As much in profile as possible, he thought that would be happier.—Yes.—He came to the top of the stairs with me, and when we bade good-night he took my hand and held it curiously as if it were something fearfully fragile, and stood and watched me down the corridor. And will you credit it? I felt inclined to run like an awkward little school-girl. I said prayers that night, thanked God—I don't quite know what for—I suppose I did then—perhaps for being happy. I looked at my foreign self in the glass too—and when the light was out. . . . Yes? . . . I did what you and every other woman might do, I cuddled my face to an imaginary face, rubbed my cheek to an imaginary cheek, whispered a God bless you! and fell asleep.

I was down before seven, paid my bill, and sat waiting, with the little tray, with its thick white cups and lumpy yellow cream before me. He came. Such a glad man, with glad eyes, glad smile, and outstretched hands. And I, I was so glad, too, that I could have shouted out for very joy of living. I might have been drinking some magic elixir instead of coffee.

'It is tiresome!' he said impatiently.

'What is tiresome? You have said that so often.'

'It is tiresome when a person one wants so

badly to keep in the country is going out of it.'

'Supposing I were to stay in it, you would probably be in one place and I in another. It is only a question of a little dearer postage!'

We both laughed at that. It takes such a little thing to make one laugh when one is happy. Then the steamer came in sight, and we walked down through the bright morning to the pier, and went on board. He stood silently. We only looked at one another. It did not then strike me as odd—it does now. The first bell rang! I felt a chill steal over me. 'It is tiresome, it is hateful!' His smile had flown; and old deep lines and traces of past suffering I had not noticed before showed plainly. . . .

'I will come back,' I said, 'when the winter is over!'

'Ay, but winter is long, or it used to be!'

'No matter, I will come with the spring!'

The second bell rang. . . . Ah, why can't we do as our hearts bid us? We have one short life, and it is spoiled by chains of our own forging, in deference to narrow custom. I shivered. There was after all an autumn chill in the air. I hate the sound of a steamer bell now. . . . The third bell. . . . We turn, and I tighten my small fingers in his great hand, and I say good-bye and God bless you! Not from a purely religious conception of God. Unless it be that God, and I think it does, means all that is good and beautiful, tender and best. I might have said 'The best I can think of befall you!' A second later and the steamer rail separates us. I look into his soul through his eyes, and see it is sorry, regretful; as sorry as I am glad it is so—he is sorry I am going from him, and in that short concentrated gaze his soul comes to me as I would have it come to me.

'When spring comes!' I whisper as I lean over to him, whilst the steamer glides out. He follows it to the end of the pier, and stands there as long as we are in sight. If he had held out his arms and said: 'Woman, stay with me!' I would, I fear, have jumped down and stayed. Didn't know anything about him! No, that is true, only that I had been waiting for something ever since I was old enough to have a want, and that he was that something, that I was nearly thirty when I found him, and . . . life is short!

I was so glad, in spite of leaving him, that I

believe I thought the sun shone differently—I almost asked some people on deck if they did not think that the day was quite the loveliest day that ever dawned since the world was a world; if there was not something peculiarly and singularly delicious in the very air? I found a quiet sofa, and lay with closed eyes and lived it over again.

The rest is more difficult to tell you. . . . I was insanely happy, then I was intensely miserable. I sent him my portrait and a letter, and counted the days and the hours to a reply. It came. I stole away to read all the warm meaning ill concealed under the words of it. Slept with it under my pillow, carried it in my bosom, and answered it straight from my heart. Why try and tell you of the aftertime? I would not go through that winter again for anything in the world. Hope, fear, suspense, joy, despondency, all the strongest feelings that can torture or wear out a heart, were mine. I longed to be up on a high mountain alone with my dream. I wonder does a man ever realise the beauty there is in a woman's thought of him. What kind were the letters? Warm, passionate, yet with a *reservatio mentalis* that hurt me, but always with a 'When spring comes!' in them. It is amazing to what depths of folly a human being can descend. I had his photograph on my table. I greeted it as a Russian peasant his household saint. . . . It would be hard to find my match in idiocy. I felt a letter coming, and waited with strained ears and fever-racked nerves for the postman's knock. Do you know there is something touchingly pitiful in the way one finds out all the tender bits in a letter and re-reads them. I have kissed a thumb-mark on the paper. Heavens, how the days dragged! I was ill with yearning thought. Night brought no rest but the comfort of being alone. All the years of my life were not as long as that weary winter. Sleep fled, and nervous pain took its place. . . . It was foolish, exceedingly foolish, because it was fatal to my looks. At the rare times I looked at myself I got a glimpse of a thin waxen yellow face with dark ringed eyes, and I was certainly older-looking. Thinking of it all dispassionately, I am inclined to believe I was hysterical. How many of the follies and frailties of women are really due to hysterical rather than moral irresponsibility, is a question. You see there is no time of sowing wild oats for women; we repress, and repress, and then some day we stumble on the man who just satisfies our sexual and emotional nature, and then there is shipwreck of some sort. When we shall live larger and freer lives, we shall be better balanced than we are now. If what I suffered is love, all I can say is I would not ask a better sample of the conventional hell's pain. Hu-s-sh! Very well, I won't say those things!

It is bad enough to be a fool and not to know it, but to be a fool and feel with every fibre of your being, every shred of your understanding that you are one, and that there is no help for it; that all your philosophy won't aid you; that you are one great want, stilled a little by a letter, only to be haunted afresh by the personality of another creature tortured with doubts and hurt by your loss of self-respect. . . . A-ah! it was a long winter! Then the New Year came and went, and time dragged slowly but surely. At length the Almanacs said it was spring-time, and the girls at the street corners called: 'vilets, sweet vilets!'; and the milliners marked down guinea bonnets to 12s. 11d., and I watched each token of its coming with a fearsome joyous expectation

. . . 'Go on,' ah yes, I'll go on, where was I? Oh, Spring was coming, wasn't it? I do not laugh as I used to, eh? How used I laugh? I forget. Well, I won't laugh if it hurts you, dear, not even at myself.

Well, once again, I was standing at a table in an hotel room waiting. It is the simple things that are so hard to describe, and that are most complicated in their effects. I said again 'Come in!' held fast to the table with my left hand and smiled—to be accurate, began a smile. Spring is later up there, perhaps some of the winter's frost was still in the atmosphere, for something froze it on my lips. I felt a curious stiffening in my face, and the touch of his hand did not thaw me. Feel happy? No, I was numb in one way and yet keenly alive to impressions. I felt as if my nerve-net was outside my skin, not under it, and that the exposure to the air and surrounding influences made it intensely, acutely sensitive. I seemed to see with my sense of feeling as well as my sight. You know how in great cold you seem to burn your hand with an icy heat if you suddenly grasp a piece of iron; well, I felt as though I was touched by glowing shivers; that sounds nonsense, but it expresses the feeling. Why? I don't know why. I was analysing, being analysed, criticising, being criticised. It was all so different, you see. Supposing you had just sipped a beaker of exhilarating, life-giving, rich wine with an exquisite bouquet, and a glow that steals through you and witches and warms you; and suddenly, without your knowing how it happens, the draught is transformed into lukewarm water, or 'Polly' without the 'dash' in it. What did he say? Let me think. Oh yes, I was wretchedly thin. Odd how things strike one. I once saw a representation of Holberg's Stundeslöse in Copenhagen. One of the characters is an ancient housekeeper, with a long money-bag, who is, as they term it, 'marriage-sick.' A match is arranged between her and a young spark in the village. The scene is this:—whilst the monetary part of the affair is being arranged by the notary, etc., he says to her:—'Permit me to pass my hand over your bosom, mistress?' She simpers, and I shall never forget the comical expression of dismay with which the suitor rolls his eyes and drops his jaw as he turns aside. I felt rather than saw the comprehensive look which accompanied his comment on my thinness, and that scene flashed across my inner vision. Odd, was it not? A sort of sympathetic after-comprehension. It was as if I, too, were having a hand passed across the flatness of my figure.

'Yes, I have got thin'—silence—had I been very ill? Yes, very! Was that why I was so pale? It was fearful, not a tinge of warm colour in my face. One would be afraid to touch me. I felt as if I were being totted up. Item, so much colour, item, so much flesh. . . . Had I been worried? I had lost that buoyant childishness that was so attractive. Ah, yes, I had dwelt too much on a trouble I had. Did I sleep? not much! That was foolish! I ought to eat plenty too. I looked as if I didn't eat enough, my eyes and cheeks were hollowed out. Ah, yes, no doubt I did look older than in Autumn! I was not contradicted. I would have told a little lie to spare a man's feelings. Men are perhaps more conscientious. What else? I am rehearsing it all as best I can. Oh, my hands were altered, he thought they were not so small, eh? . . . Might be my wrists were less round, that made a difference! Did it? They certainly were larger, and not so white. . . . Did he kiss me? Oh, yes. You see I wanted to sift this thing thoroughly to get clear into my head what ground I was standing on. So I let him. They were merely lip kisses; his spirit did not come to mine, and I was simply analysing them all the time. Did I not feel anything? Yes, I did, deeply hurt. Ah, I can't say how they hurt me; they lacked everything a kiss, as the expression of the strongest, best feeling of a man and woman, *can* hold. How do I know? My dear woman, have you never dreamt, felt, had *intuitive experiences*? I have. I am not sure that I had not a keen sense of the ludicrous side of the whole affair, that one portion of my soul was not having a laugh at the other's expense. I do not quite know what I had been expecting. 'Tis true he had written me beautiful letters. You see he is too much of a word-artist to write anything else. Treated me badly? . . . No, I am not prepared to say that he did. I am glad he was too honest to hide his startled realisation of the fact that Autumn and Spring are different seasons, and that one's feelings may undergo a change in a winter. I do not see why I should resent that. Why, it would be punishing him for having cared for me. To put it in his words: 'I came as a strangely lovely dream into his life.' Probably the whole mistake lay in that. He thought of me as a dream lady with dainty hands, idealised me—and wrote to the dream creature. When I came back in the flesh, he realised that I was a prosaic fact, with less charming hands, a tendency to leanness, and coming crow's feet. His look of dismayed awakening was simply delicious. I wish I could catch and fasten the fleeting images that flit across my memory, you would grasp my mental attitude better. In the midst of all my pain, I was sitting next him, and he was stroking my hand mechanically, I noticed a glass case on the wall containing an Italian landscape with ball-blue sky and pink lakes. Pasteboard figures of Dutch-peasant build, with Zouave jackets, Tyrolese hats, and bandaged legs, figured in the foreground. You wound it up, and the figures danced to a *varsoviana*. I was listening to him, and yet at the same time

I caught myself imagining how he and I would look dressed like that, bobbing about to the old-fashioned tune. I could hardly keep from shrieking with laughter. He had a turn-down collar on ; he ought always to wear unstarched linen—it and his throat didn't fit. You cannot understand me ? Dearest woman, I do not pretend to understand the thing myself.

Did we not talk about anything ? Of course we did. Tolstoi and his doctrine of celibacy. Ibsen's Hedda. Strindberg's view of the female animal. And we agreed that Friedrich Nietzche appealed to us immensely. You must make allowances. Here was a man passionately attached to his art. His art that he had been treating churlishly for months, for the sake of a dream. The dream was out, and he feared her revenge. That is the one potent element of consolation for me. If one has made an idiot of one's-self, it is at least self-consoling to have done so for a genius. He chose the better part, if you come to think of it. The man or woman who jeopardises a great talent, be it of writing, painting, or acting for marriage's sake, is bartering a precious birthright for a mess of pottage—mostly indifferent pottage. And even if it were excellent, it is bound to pall, when one has it every day. There never was a marriage yet in which one was not a loser; and it is generally the more gifted half who has to pay the heavier toll. . . . I believe he was intensely sorry for me; I asked him once you know, half playfully, half maliciously, if he had meant something; something deliciously tender which I quoted out of one of his letters. He paled to his lips, closed his eyes for a second, and I saw drops of sweat break out on his forehead. I sprang up and turned aside his answer. I remember when I was a little child I never would pick a flower. I always fancied they felt it and bled to death. I used to sneak behind and gather up all those my playmates threw down on the road or fields, and put them, stalks down, into the water in the ditch or brook—even now I can't wear them. I did not wish to hurt him either, he could not help his passion-flower withering. I suppose it was written that my love should turn, like fairy gold, into withered leaves in my grasp . . . What, dear? a white hair! oh, I saw several lately. How did it end? Oh, he said that he was going away to glean material for a new book; that he would burn my letters; it was safer and wiser to burn letters. No, I did not ask him, he volunteered it. He asked me, did I not think so? I said Yes. But is it not marvellous how dazzlingly swift our thoughts can travel; like light. Whilst I was saying 'yes,' one often regretted not having burned letters; receipts, receipts for bills were really the only things of importance to keep. I was thinking and crying inwardly over my letters. Such letters. One only writes once like that, I think. All the perfume of the flowers I ever smelt, all the sun-glints on hill and sea, all the strains of music and light and love I had garnered from the glad fresh young years, when I tossed cowslip balls in the meadows, were crystallised into love-words in those letters of mine. It seemed to me often that the words burnt with a white flame as I wrote them, and I was shy when I saw them written. And he said: 'I shall burn them!' much as you might say: 'I shall take the trimming off that last summer hat of mine.' I did not like to think of his burning them, perhaps with his old washing bills. Do you know, if I had a finger or toe cut off, I wouldn't like them to take it away, I'd like to bury it. A sort of feel, I suppose. . . . Well, we said good-bye! I felt as if I had a sponge with a lot of holes in it, instead of a heart, and that all the feeling had oozed away through them. He was glad to go, I think; he felt a brute, I daresay, yet how could he help it?

* * * * *

Were you ever at the Scandinavian church in the Docks? I went one Sunday after I came back. I like those blue-eyed, seafaring folk; and the priest wears a black gown and stiff ruff like Luther of mixed renown. An apple-tree outside the open door was struggling to open its delicate pink blossoms; each petal had a tinge of soot; it reminded me of the pretty cheeks of a grimy maid-of-all-work. I sat still. A sunbeam came in and pierced Judas's heart, as he sat at his section of the Last Supper table, and it wrapped me up in a sun haze, so that all was misty around me. The sermon only struck my ear with a soothing, drowsy roll, something like the wave-note of the in-curling sea in the Mediterranean, a *legato* accompaniment to my thoughts; and I had a grand burial all by myself. I dug a deep grave and laid all my dreams and foolish wishes and sweet hopes in it. A puff of wind rustled through the riggings of the ships and set the flags with their yellow cross fluttering, and scattered a few of the tender blooms over it . . . and, ah well . . . it seems hard to realise now Spring has gone!

Do you really think that crinolines will be worn?

THE SPELL OF THE WHITE ELF

HAVE you ever read out a joke that seemed excruciatingly funny, or repeated a line of poetry that struck you as being inexpressibly tender, and found that your listener was not impressed as you were? I have, and so it may be that this will bore you, though it was momentous enough to me.

I had been up in Norway to receive a little legacy that fell to me, and though my summer visits were not infrequent, I had never been up there in mid-winter, at least not since I was a little child tobogganing with Hans Jörgen (Hans Jörgen Dahl is his full name), and that was long ago. We are connected. Hans Jörgen and I were both orphans, and a cousin—we called her aunt—was one of our guardians. He was her favourite; and when an uncle on my mother's side—she was Cornish born; my father, a ship captain, met her at Dartmouth—offered to take me, I think she was glad to let me go. I was a lanky girl of eleven, and Hans Jörgen and I were sweethearts. We were to be married some day, we had arranged all that, and he reminded me of it when I was going away, and gave me a silver perfume box, with a gilt crown on top, that had belonged to his mother. And later when he was going to America he came to see me first; he was a long freckled hobbledehoy, with just the same true eyes and shock head. I was, I thought, quite grown up, I had passed my 'intermediate' and was condescending as girls are. But I don't think it impressed Hans Jörgen much, for he gave me a little ring, turquoise forget-me-nots with enamelled leaves and a motto inside—a quaint old thing that belonged to a sainted aunt—they keep things a long time in Norway—and said he would send for me; but of course I laughed at that. He has grown to be a great man out in Cincinnati and waits always. I wrote later and told him I thought marriage a vocation and I hadn't one for it; but Hans Jörgen took no notice; just said he'd wait. He understands waiting, I'll say that for Hans Jörgen.

I have been alone now for five years, working away, though I was left enough to keep me before. Somehow I have not the same gladness in my work of late years. Working for one's-self seems a poor end even if one puts by money. But this has little or nothing to do with the white elf, has it?

Christiania is a singular city if one knows how to see under the surface, and I enjoyed my stay there greatly. The Hull boat was to sail at 4.30, and I had sent my things down early, for I was to dine at the Grand at two with a cousin, a typical Christiania man. It was a fine clear day, and Karl Johann was thronged with folks. The band was playing in the park, and pretty girls and laughing students walked up and down. Every one who is anybody may generally be seen about that time. Henrik Ibsen—if you did not know him from his portrait, you would take him to be a prosperous merchant—was going home to dine; but Björnstjerne Björnson, in town just then, with his grand leonine head, and the kind, keen eyes behind his glasses, was standing near the Storthing House with a group of politicians, probably discussing the vexed question of separate consulship. In no city does one see such characteristic odd faces and such queerly cut clothes. The streets are full of students. The farmers' sons amongst them are easily recognised by their homespun, sometimes home-made suits, their clever heads and intelligent faces; from them come the writers, and brain carriers of Norway. The Finns, too, have a distinctive type of head and a something elusive in the expression of their changeful eyes. But all, the town students, too, of easier manners and slangier tongues—all alike are going, as finances permit, to dine in restaurant or steam-kitchen. I saw the *menu* for to-day posted up outside the door of the latter as I passed—'Rice porridge and salt meat soup, 6d.,' and Hans Jörgen came back with a vivid picture of childhood days, when every family in the little coast-town where we lived had a fixed *menu* for every day in the week; and it was quite a distinction to have meat balls on pickled herring day, or ale soup when all the folks in town were cooking omelettes with bacon. How he used to eat rice porridge in those days! I can see him now put his heels together and give his awkward bow as he said, 'Tak for Maden tante!' Well, we are sitting in the

Grand *Café* after dinner, at a little table near the door, watching the people pass in and out. An ubiquitous 'sample-count' from Berlin is measuring his wits with a young Norwegian merchant; he is standing green chartreuse; it pays to be generous even for a German, when you can oust honest Leeds cloth with German shoddy. At least so my cousin says. He knows every one by sight, and points out all the celebrities to me. Suddenly he bows profoundly. I look round. A tall woman with very square shoulders, and gold-rimmed spectacles is passing us with two gentlemen. She is English by her tailor-made gown and little shirt-front, and noticeable anywhere.

'That lady,' says my cousin, 'is a compatriot of yours. She is a very fine person, a very learned lady; she has been looking up referats in the university bibliothek. Professor Sturm—he is a good friend of me—did tell me. I forget her name; she is married. I suppose her husband he stay at home and keep the house!'

My cousin has just been refused by a young lady dentist, who says she is too comfortably off to change for a small housekeeping business, so I excuse his sarcasm. We leave as the time draws on and sleigh down to the steamer. I like the jingle of the bells, and I feel a little sad. There is a witchery about the country that creeps into one and works like a love-philter, and if one has once lived up there, one never gets it out of one's blood again. I go on board and lean over and watch the people. There are a good many for winter-time. The bell rings. Two sleighs drive up and my compatriot and her friends appear. She shakes hands with them and comes leisurely up the gangway. The thought flits through me that she would cross it in just that cool way if she were facing death ; it is foolish, but most of our passing thoughts are just as inconsequent. She calls down a remembrance to some one in such pretty Norwegian, much prettier than mine, and then we swing round. Handkerchiefs wave in every hand, never have I seen such persistent handkerchief-waving as at the departure of a boat in Norway. It is a national characteristic. If you live at the mouth of a fjord, and go to the market town at the head of it for your weekly supply of coffee beans, the population give you a 'send off' with fluttering kerchiefs. It is as universal as the 'Thanks.' Hans Jörgen says I am anglicised and only see the ridiculous side, forgetting the kind feelings that prompt it. I find a strange pleasure in watching the rocks peep out under the snow, the children dragging their hand-sleds along the ice. All the little bits of winter life of which I get flying glimpses as we pass, bring back scenes grown dim in the years between. There is a mist ahead; and when we pass Dröbak cuddled like a dormouse for winter's sleep I go below. A bright coal fire burns in the open grate of the stove, and the *Rollo* saloon looks very cosy. My compatriot is stretched in a big arm-chair reading. She is sitting comfortably with one leg crossed over the other, in the manner called 'shockingly unladylike' of my early lessons in deportment. The flame flickers over the patent leather of her neat low-heeled boot, and strikes a spark from the pin in her tie. There is something manlike about her. I don't know where it lies, but it is there. Her hair curls in grey flecked rings about her head; it has not a cut look, seems rather to grow short naturally. She has a charming tubbed look. Of course every lady is alike clean, but some men and women have an individual look of sweet cleanness that is a beauty of itself. She feels my gaze and looks up and smiles. She has a rare smile, it shows her white teeth and softens her features:

'The fire is cosy, isn't it? I hope we shall have an easy passage, so that it can be kept in.'

I answer something in English.

She has a trick of wrinkling her brows, she does it now as she says:

'A-ah, I should have said you were Norsk. Are you not really? Surely you have a typical head, or eyes and hair at the least?'

'Half of me is Norsk, but I have lived a long time in England.'

'Father of course; case of "there was a sailor loved a lass," was it not?'

I smile an assent and add: 'I lost them both when I was very young.'

A reflective look steals over her face. It is stern in repose; and as she seems lost in some train of thought of her own I go to my cabin and lie down; the rattling noises and the smell of paint makes me feel ill. I do not go out again. I wake next morning with a sense of fear at the stillness. There is no sound but a lapping wash of water at the side of the steamer, but it is delicious to lie quietly after the vibration of the screw and the sickening swing. I look at my watch; seven o'clock. I cannot make out why there is such a silence, as we only stop at Christiansand long enough to take cargo and passengers. I dress and go out. The saloon is empty but the fire is burning brightly. I go to the pantry and ask the stewardess when we arrived? Early, she says; all the passengers for here are already gone on shore; and there is a thick fog outside, goodness knows how long we'll be kept. I go to the top of the stairs and look out; the prospect is uninviting and I come down again and turn over some books on the table; in Russian, I think. I feel sure they are hers.

'Good-morning!' comes her pleasant voice. How alert and bright-eyed she is! It is a pick-me-up to look at her.

'You did not appear last night? Not given in already, I hope!'

She is kneeling on one knee before the fire, holding her palms to the glow, and with her figure hidden in her loose, fur-lined coat and the light showing up her strong face under the little tweed cap, she seems so like a clever-faced slight man, that I feel I am conventionally guilty in talking so freely to her. She looks at me with a deliberate critical air, and then springs up.

'Let me give you something for your head! Stewardess, a wine-glass!'

I should not dream of remonstrance—not if she were to command me to drink sea-water; and I am not complaisant as a rule.

When she comes back I swallow it bravely, but I leave some powder in the glass; she shakes her head, and I finish this too. We sat and talked, or at least she talked and I listened. I don't remember what she said, I only know that she was making clear to me most of the things that had puzzled me for a long time; questions that arise in silent hours; that one speculates over, and to which one finds no answer in text-books. How she knew just the subjects that worked in me I knew not; some subtle intuitive sympathy, I suppose, enabled her to find it out. It was the same at breakfast, she talked down to the level of the men present (of course they did not see that it might be possible for a woman to do that), and made it a very pleasant meal.

It was in the evening—we had the saloon to ourselves—when she told me about the white elf. I had been talking of myself and of Hans Jörgen.

'I like your Mr. Hans Jörgen,' she said, 'he has a strong nature and knows what he wants; there is reliability in him. They are rarer qualities than one thinks in men, I have found through life that the average man is weaker than we are. It must be a good thing to have a stronger nature to lean to. I have never had that.'

There is a want in the tone of her voice as she ends, and I feel inclined to put out my hand and stroke hers—she has beautiful long hands—but I am afraid to do so. I query shyly—

'Have you no little ones?'

'Children, you mean? No, I am one of the barren ones; they are less rare than they used to be. But I have a white elf at home and that makes up for it. Shall I tell you how the elf came? Well, its mother is a connection of mine, and she hates me with an honest hatred. It is the only honest feeling I ever discovered in her. It was about the time that she found the elf was to come that it broke out openly, but that was mere coincidence. How she detested me! Those narrow, poor natures are capable of an intensity of feeling concentrated on one object that larger natures can scarcely measure. Now I shall tell you something strange. I do not pretend to understand it, I may have my theory, but that is of no physiological value, I only tell it to you. Well, all the time she was carrying the elf she was full of simmering hatred and she wished me evil often enough. One feels those things in an odd way. Why did she? Oh, that . . . that was a family affair, with perhaps a thread of jealousy mixed up in the knot. Well, one day the climax came, and much was said, and I went away and married and got ill and the doctors said I would be childless. And in the meantime the little human soul—I thought about it so often—had fought its way out of the darkness. We childless women weave more fancies into the "mithering o' bairns" than the actual mothers themselves. The poetry of it is not spoilt by nettle-rash or chin-cough any more than our figures. I am a writer by profession—oh, you knew! No, hardly celebrated, but I put my little chips into the great mosaic as best I can. Positions are reversed, they often are now-a-days. My husband stays at home and grows good things to eat, and pretty things to look at, and I go out and win bread and butter. It is a matter not of who has most brains, but whose brains are most saleable. Fit in with the housekeeping? Oh yes. I have a treasure, too, in Belinda. She is one of those women who must have something to love. She used to love cats, birds, dogs, anything. She is one bump of philo-progenitiveness, but she hates men. She says: "If one could only have a child, ma'm, without a husband or the disgrace; ugh, the disgusting men!" Do you know I think that is not an uncommon feeling amongst a certain number of women. I have often drawn her out on the subject. It struck me, because I have often found it in other women. I have known many, particularly older women, who would give anything in God's world to have a child of "their own" if it could be got just as Belinda says, "without the horrid man or the shame." It seems congenital with some women to have deeply rooted in their innermost nature a smouldering enmity, ay, sometimes a physical disgust to men, it is a kind of kin-feeling to the race dislike of white men to black. Perhaps it explains why woman, where her own feelings are not concerned, will always make common cause with woman against him. I have often thought about it. You should hear Belinda's "serve him right" when some fellow comes to grief. I have a little of it myself (meditatively), but in a broader way, you know. I like to cut them out in their own province. Well, the elf was born, and now comes the singular part of it. It was a wretched, frail little being with a startling likeness to me. It was as if the evil the mother had wished me had worked on the child, and the constant thought of me stamped my features on its little face. I was working then on a Finland saga, and I do not know why it was, but the thought of that little being kept disturbing my work. It was worst in the afternoon time when the house seemed quietest; there is always a lull then outside and inside. Have you ever noticed that? The birds hush their singing and the work is done. Belinda used to sit sewing in the kitchen, and the words of a hymn she used to lilt in half tones, something about 'joy bells ringing, children singing,' floated in to me, and the very tick-tock of the old clock sounded like the rocking of wooden cradles. It made me think sometimes that it would be pleasant to hear small pattering feet and the call of voices through the silent house. And I suppose it acted as an irritant on my imaginative faculty, for the whole room seemed filled with the spirits of little children. They seemed to dance round me with uncertain, lightsome steps, waving tiny pink dimpled hands, shaking sunny flossy curls, and haunting me with their great innocent child-eyes; filled with the unconscious sadness and the infinite questioning that is oftenest seen in the gaze of children. I used to fancy something stirred in me, and the spirits of unborn little ones never to come to life in me troubled me. I was probably overworked at the time. How we women digress! I am telling you more about myself than my white elf. Well, trouble came to their home, and I went and offered to take it. It was an odd little thing, and when I looked at it I could see how like we were. My glasses dimmed somehow, and a lump kept rising in my throat, when it smiled up out of its great eyes and held out two bits of hands like shrivelled white rose leaves. Such a tiny scrap it was; it was not bigger, she said, than a baby of eleven months. I suppose they can tell that as I can the date of a dialect; but I am getting wiser,' with an emotional softening of her face and quite a proud look. 'A child is like one of those wonderful runic alphabets; the signs are simple but the lore they contain is marvellous. "She is very like you," said the mother. "Hold her." She was only beginning to walk. I did. You never saw such elfin ears with strands of silk floss ringing round them, and the quaintest, darlingest wrinkles in its forehead, two long, and one short, just as I have,' putting her head forward for me to see. 'The other children were strong, and the one on the road she hoped would be healthy. So I took it there and then, "clothes and baby, cradle and all." Yes, I have a collection of nursery rhymes from many nations; I was going to put them in a book, but I say them to the elf now. I wired to my husband. You should have seen me going home. I was so nervous, I was not half as nervous when I read my paper—it was rather a celebrated paper, perhaps you heard of it—to the Royal Geographical Society. It was on Esquimaux marriage songs, and the analogy between them and the Song of Solomon. She was so light, and so wrapped up, and my *pince-nez* kept dropping off when I stooped over her—I got spectacles after that—and I used to fancy I had dropped her out of the wrappings, and peep under the shawl to make sure'—with a sick shiver —' to find her sucking her thumb. And I nearly passed my station. And then a valuable book—indeed, it is really a case of MSS., and almost unique—I had borrowed for reference with some trouble, could not be found, and my husband roared with laughter when it turned up in the cradle. Belinda was at the gate anxious to take her, and he said I did not know how to hold her, that I was holding her like a book of notes at a lecture, and so I gave her to Belinda. I think the poor little thing found it all strange, and when she puckered up her face, and thrust out her under lip, and two great tears jumped off her lashes, we all felt ready for hanging. But Belinda, though she doesn't know one language, not even her own, for she sows her h's broadcast and picks them up at hazard, she *can* talk to a baby. I am so glad for that reason she is bigger now; I couldn't manage it, I could not reason out any system they go on in baby talk. I tried mixing up the tenses, but somehow it wasn't right. My husband says it is not more odd than salmon taking a fly that is certainly like nothing they ever see in nature. Anyway it answered splendidly. Belinda used to say—I made a note of some of them—"Didsum was denn? Oo did! Was ums de prettiest itta sweetums denn? oo was. An' did um put 'em in a nasty shawl an' joggle 'em in an ole puff-puff, um did, was a shame! Hitchy cum, hitchy cum, hitchy cum hi, Chinaman no likey me!" This always made her laugh, though in what connection the Chinaman came in I never *could* fathom. I was a little jealous of Belinda, but she knew how to undress her. George, that's my husband's name, said the bath water was too hot, and that the proper way to test it was to put one's elbow in. Belinda laughed, but I must confess it did feel too hot when I tried it that way; but how did he know? I got her such pretty clothes, I was going to buy a pragtbind of Nietzsche, but that must wait. George made her a cot with her name carved on the head of it, such a pretty one.'

'Did you find she made a change in your lives?' I asked.

'Oh, didn't she! Children are such funny things. I stole away to have a look at her later on, and did not hear him come after me. She looked so sweet, and she was smiling in her sleep. I believe the Irish peasantry say that an angel is whispering when a baby does that. I had given up all belief myself, except the belief in a Creator who is working out some system that is too infinite for our finite minds to grasp. If one looks round with seeing eyes one can't help thinking that after a run of 1893 years, Christianity is not very consoling in its results. But at that moment, kneeling next the cradle, I felt a strange, solemn feeling stealing over me; one is conscious of the same effect in a grand cathedral filled with the peal of organ music and soaring voices. It was as if all the old, sweet, untroubled child-belief came back for a spell, and I wondered if far back in the Nazarene village Mary ever knelt and watched the Christ-child sleep; and the legend of how he was often seen to weep but never to smile came back to me, and I think the sorrow I felt as I thought was an act of contrition and faith. I could not teach a child scepticism, so I remembered my husband prayed, and I resolved to ask him to teach her. You see (half hesitatingly) I have more brains, or at least more intellectuality than my husband, and in that case one is apt to undervalue simpler, perhaps greater, qualities. That came home to me, and I began to cry, I don't know why, and he lifted me up, and I think I said something of the kind to him. . . . We got nearer to one another someway. He said it was unlucky to cry over a child.

'It made such a difference in the evenings. I used to hurry home—I was on the staff of the *World's Review* just then—and it was so jolly to see the quaint little phiz smile up when I went in.

'Belinda was quite jealous of George. She said "Master worritted in an" out, an' interfered with everything, she never seen a man as knew so much about babies, not for one as never 'ad none of 'is own. Wot if he didn't go to Parkins hisself, an' say as how she was to have the milk of one cow, an' mind not mix it." I wish you could have seen the insinuating distrust on Belinda's face. I laughed. I believe we were all getting too serious, I know I felt years younger. I told George that it was really suspicious ; how did he acquire such a stock of baby lore ? *I* hadn't any. It was all very well to say Aunt Mary's kids. I should never be surprised if I saw a Zwazi woman appear with a lot of tawny pickaninnies in tow. George was shocked—I often shock him.

'She began to walk as soon as she got stronger. I never saw such an inquisitive mite. I had to rearrange all my bookshelves, change Le Nu de Rabelais, after Garnier, you know, and several others from the lower shelves to the top ones. One can't be so Bohemian when there is a little white soul like that playing about, can one? When we are alone she always comes in to say her prayers, and good-night. Larry Moore of the *Vulture*—he is one of the most wickedly amusing of men, prides himself on being *fin de siècle*—don't you detest that word?—or nothing, raves about Dégas, and is a worshipper of the decadent school of verse, quotes Verlaine, you know—well, he came in one evening on his way to some music hall. She's a whimsical little thing, not without incipient coquetry either; well, she would say them to him. If you can imagine a masher of the Jan van Beer type bending his head to hear a child in a white "nighty" lisping prayers, you have an idea of the picture. She kissed him good-night too; she never would before; and he must have forgotten his engagement, for he stayed with us to supper. She rules us all with a touch of her little hands, and I fancy we are all the better for it. Would you like to see her?' She hands me a medallion, with a beautifully painted head in it. I can't say she is a pretty child, a weird, elf-like thing, with questioning, wistful eyes, and masses of dark hair; and yet as I look the little face draws me to it, and makes a kind of yearning in me; strikes me with a 'fairy blast' perhaps.

The journey was all too short, and when we got to Hull she saw me to my train. It was odd to see the quiet way in which she got everything she wanted. She put me into the carriage, got me a footwarmer and a magazine, kissed me and said as she held my hand, 'The world is small, we run in circles, perhaps we shall meet again, in any case I wish you a white elf.' I was sorry to part with her; I felt richer than before I knew her; I fancy she goes about the world giving graciously from her richer nature to the poorer-endowed folks she meets on her way.

Often since that night I have rounded my arm and bowed down my face and fancied I had a little human elf cuddled to my breast.

* * * *

I am very busy just now getting everything ready; I had so much to buy. I don't like confessing it even to myself, but down in the bottom of my deepest trunk I have laid a parcel of things, such pretty tiny things. I saw them at a sale, I couldn't resist them, they were so cheap; even if one doesn't want the things, it seems a sin to let them go. Besides, there may be some poor woman out in Cincinnati. I wrote to Hans Jörgen, you know, back in spring, and . . . . Du störer Gud! There is Hans Jörgen coming across the street.

A LITTLE GREY GLOVE.

EARLY-SPRING, 1893.

'The book of life begins with a man and woman in a garden and ends—with Revelations.' OSCAR WILDE.

YES, most fellows' book of life may be said to begin at the chapter where woman comes in; mine did. She came in years ago, when I was a raw undergraduate. With the sober thought of retrospective analysis, I may say she was not all my fancy painted her; indeed now that I come to think of it there was no fancy about the vermeil of her cheeks, rather an artificial reality; she had her bower in the bar of the Golden Boar, and I was madly in love with her, seriously intent on lawful wedlock. Luckily for me she threw me over for a neighbouring pork butcher, but at the time I took it hardly, and it made me sex-shy. I was a very poor man in those days. One feels one's griefs more keenly then, one hasn't the wherewithal to buy distraction. Besides, ladies snubbed me rather, on the rare occasions I met them. Later

I fell in for a legacy, the forerunner of several; indeed, I may say I am beastly rich. My tastes are simple too, and I haven't any poor relations. I believe they are of great assistance in getting rid of superfluous capital, wish I had some! It was after the legacy that women discovered my attractions. They found that there was something superb in my plainness (before, they said ugliness), something after the style of the late Victor Emanuel, something infinitely more striking than mere ordinary beauty. At least so Harding told me his sister said, and she had the reputation of being a clever girl. Being an only child, I never had the opportunity other fellows had of studying the undress side of women through familiar intercourse, say with sisters. Their most ordinary belongings were sacred to me. I had, I used to be told, ridiculous high-flown notions about them (by the way I modified those considerably on closer acquaintance). I ought to study them, nothing like a woman for developing a fellow. So I laid in a stock of books in different languages, mostly novels, in which women played title rôles, in order to get up some definite data before venturing amongst them. I can't say I derived much benefit from this course. There seemed to be as great a diversity of opinion about the female species as, let us say, about the salmonidæ.

My friend Ponsonby Smith, who is one of the oldest fly-fishers in the three kingdoms, said to me once: 'Take my word for it, there are only four true salmo; the salar, the trutta, the fario, the ferox; all the rest are just varieties, sub-genuses of the above; stick to that. Some writing fellow divided all the women into good-uns and bad-uns. But as a conscientious stickler for truth, I must say that both in trout as in women, I have found myself faced with most puzzling varieties, that were a tantalising blending of several qualities.' I then resolved to study them on my own account. I pursued the Eternal Feminine in a spirit of purely scientific investigation. I knew you'd laugh sceptically at that, but it's a fact. I was impartial in my selection of subjects for observation,—French, German, Spanish, as well as the home product. Nothing in petticoats escaped me. I devoted myself to the freshest *ingenue* as well as the experienced widow of three departed; and I may as well confess that the more I saw of her, the less I understood her. But I think they understood me. They refused to take me *au sérieux*. When they weren't fleecing me, they were interested in the state of my soul (I preferred the former), but all humbugged me equally, so I gave them up. I took to rod and gun instead, *pro salute animæ*; it's decidedly safer. I have scoured every country in the globe; indeed I can say that I have shot and fished in woods and waters where no other white man, perhaps, ever dropped a beast or played a fish before. There is no life like the life of a free wanderer, and no lore like the lore one gleans in the great book of nature. But one must have freed one's spirit from the taint of the town before one can even read the alphabet of its mystic meaning.

What has this to do with the glove? True, not much, and yet it has a connection—it accounts for me.

Well, for twelve years I have followed the impulses of the wandering spirit that dwells in me. I have seen the sun rise in Finland and gild the Devil's Knuckles as he sank behind the Drachensberg. I have caught the barba and the gamer yellow fish in the Vaal river, taken muskelunge and black-bass in Canada, thrown a fly over *guapote* and *cavallo* in Central American lakes, and choked the monster eels of the Mauritius with a cunningly faked-up duckling. But I have been shy as a chub at the shadow of a woman.

Well, it happened last year I came back on business—another confounded legacy; end of June too, just as I was off to Finland. But Messrs. Thimble and Rigg, the highly respectable firm who look after my affairs, represented that I owed it to others, whom I kept out of their share of the legacy, to stay near town till affairs were wound up. They told me, with a view to reconcile me perhaps, of a trout stream with a decent inn near it; an unknown stream in Kent. It seems a junior member of the firm is an angler, at least he sometimes catches pike or perch in the Medway some way from the stream where the trout rise in audacious security from artificial lures. I stipulated for a clerk to come down with any papers to be signed, and started at once for Victoria. I decline to tell the name of my find, firstly because the trout are the gamest little fish that ever rose to fly and run to a good two pounds. Secondly, I have paid for all the rooms in the inn for the next year, and I want it to myself. The glove is lying on the table next me as I write. If it isn't in my breast-pocket or under my pillow, it is in some place where I can see it. It has a delicate grey body (Suède, I think they call it) with a whipping of silver round the top, and a darker grey silk tag to fasten it. It is marked 5¾ inside, and has a delicious scent about it, to keep off moths, I suppose; naphthaline is better. It reminds me of a 'silver-sedge' tied on a ten hook. I startled the good landlady of the little inn (there is no village fortunately) when I arrived with the only porter of the tiny station laden with traps. She hesitated about a private sitting-room, but eventually we compromised matters, as I was willing to share it with the other visitor. I got into knickerbockers at once, collared a boy to get me worms and minnow for the morrow, and as I felt too lazy to unpack tackle, just sat in the shiny arm-chair (made comfortable by the successive sitting of former occupants) at the open window and looked out. The river, not the trout stream, winds to the right, and the trees cast trembling shadows into its clear depths. The red tiles of a farm roof show between the beeches, and break the monotony of blue sky background. A dusty waggoner is slaking his thirst with a tankard of ale. I am conscious of the strange lonely feeling that a visit to England always gives me. Away in strange lands, even in solitary places, one doesn't feel it somehow. One is filled with the hunter's lust, bent on a 'kill;' but at home in the quiet country, with the smoke curling up from some fireside, the mowers busy laying the hay in swaths, the children tumbling under the trees in the orchards, and a girl singing as she spreads the clothes on the sweetbrier hedge, amidst a scene quick with home sights and sounds, a strange lack creeps in and makes itself felt in a dull, aching way. Oddly enough, too, I had a sense of uneasiness, a 'something going to happen.' I had often experienced it when out alone in a great forest, or on an unknown lake, and it always meant 'ware danger' of some kind. But why should I feel it here? Yet I did, and I couldn't shake it off. I took to examining the room. It was a commonplace one of the usual type. But there was a work-basket on the table, a dainty thing, lined with blue satin. There was a bit of lace stretched over shiny blue linen, with the needle sticking in it; such fairy work, like cobwebs seen from below, spun from a branch against a background of sky. A gold thimble, too, with initials, not the landlady's, I know. What pretty things, too, in the basket! A scissors, a capital shape for fly-making; a little file, and some floss silk and tinsel, the identical colour I want for a new fly I have in my head, one that will be a demon to kill. The northern devil I mean to call him. Some one looks in behind me, and a light step passes up-stairs. I drop the basket, I don't know why. There are some reviews near it. I take up one, and am soon buried in an article on Tasmanian fauna. It is strange, but whenever I do know anything about a subject, I always find these writing fellows either entirely ignorant or damned wrong.

After supper, I took a stroll to see the river. It was a silver grey evening, with just the last lemon and pink streaks of the sunset staining the sky. There had been a shower, and somehow the smell of the dust after rain mingled with the mignonette in the garden brought back vanished scenes of small-boyhood, when I caught minnows in a bottle, and dreamt of a shilling rod as happiness unattainable. I turned aside from the road in accordance with directions, and walked towards the stream. Holloa! some one before me, what a bore! The angler is hidden by an elder-bush, but I can see the fly drop delicately, artistically on the water. Fishing up-stream, too! There is a bit of broken water there, and the midges dance in myriads; a silver gleam, and the line spins out, and the fly falls just in the right place. It is growing dusk, but the fellow is an adept at quick, fine casting—I wonder what fly he has on—why, he's going to try down-stream now? I hurry forward, and as I near him, I swerve to the left out of the way. S-s-s-s! a sudden sting in the lobe of my ear. Hey! I cry as I find I am caught; the tail fly is fast in it. A slight, grey-clad woman holding the rod lays it carefully down and comes towards me through the gathering dusk. My first impulse is to snap the gut and take to my heels, but I am held by something less tangible but far more powerful than the grip of the Limerick hook in my ear.

'I am very sorry!' she says in a voice that matched the evening, it was so quiet and soft; 'but it was exceedingly stupid of you to come behind like that.'

'I didn't think you threw such a long line; I thought I was safe,' I stammered.

'Hold this!' she says, giving me a diminutive fly-book, out of which she has taken a scissors. I obey meekly. She snips the gut.

'Have you a sharp knife? If I strip the hook you can push it through; it is lucky it isn't in the cartilage.'

I suppose I am an awful idiot, but I only handed her the knife, and she proceeded as calmly as if stripping a hook in a man's ear were an everyday occurrence. Her gown is of some soft grey stuff, and her grey leather belt is silver clasped. Her hands are soft and cool and steady, but there is a rarely disturbing thrill in their gentle touch. The thought flashed through my mind that I had just missed that, a woman's voluntary tender touch, not a paid caress, all my life.

'Now you can push it through yourself. I

hope it won't hurt much.' Taking the hook, I push it through, and a drop of blood follows it. 'Oh!' she cries, but I assure her it is nothing, and stick the hook surreptitiously in my coat sleeve. Then we both laugh, and I look at her for the first time. She has a very white forehead, with little tendrils of hair blowing round it under her grey cap, her eyes are grey. I didn't see that then, I only saw they were steady, smiling eyes that matched her mouth. Such a mouth, the most maddening mouth a man ever longed to kiss, above a too pointed chin, soft as a child's; indeed, the whole face looks soft in the misty light.

'I am sorry I spoilt your sport!' I say.

'Oh, that don't matter, it's time to stop. I got two brace, one a beauty.'

She is winding in her line, and I look in her basket; they *are* beauties, one two-pounder, the rest running from a half to a pound.

'What fly?'

'Yellow dun took that one, but your assailant was a partridge spider.' I sling her basket over my shoulder; she takes it as a matter of course, and we retrace our steps. I feel curiously happy as we walk towards the road; there is a novel delight in her nearness; the feel of woman works subtly and strangely in me; the rustle of her skirt as it brushes the black-heads in the meadow-grass, and the delicate perfume, partly violets, partly herself, that comes to me with each of her movements is a rare pleasure. I am hardly surprised when she turns into the garden of the inn, I think I knew from the first that she would.

'Better bathe that ear of yours, and put a few drops of carbolic in the water.' She takes the basket as she says it, and goes into the kitchen. I hurry over this, and go into the little sitting-room. There is a tray with a glass of milk and some oaten cakes upon the table. I am too disturbed to sit down; I stand at the window and watch the bats flitter in the gathering moonlight, and listen with quivering nerves for her step—perhaps she will send for the tray, and not come after all. What a fool I am to be disturbed by a grey-clad witch with a tantalising mouth! That comes of loafing about doing nothing. I mentally darn the old fool who saved her money instead of spending it. Why the devil should I be bothered? I don't want it anyhow. She comes in as I fume, and I forget everything at her entrance. I push the arm-chair towards the table, and she sinks quietly into it, pulling the tray nearer. She has a wedding ring on, but somehow it never strikes me to wonder if she is married or a widow or who she may be. I am content to watch her break her biscuits. She has the prettiest hands, and a trick of separating her last fingers when she takes hold of anything. They remind me of white orchids I saw somewhere. She led me to talk ; about Africa, I think. I liked to watch her eyes glow deeply in the shadow and then catch light as she bent forward to say something in her quick responsive way.

'Long ago when I was a girl,' she said once.

'Long ago?' I echo incredulously, 'surely not?'

'Ah, but yes, you haven't seen me in the daylight,' with a soft little laugh. 'Do you know what the gipsies say? "Never judge a woman or a ribbon by candle-light." They might have said moonlight equally well.'

She rises as she speaks, and I feel an overpowering wish to have her put out her hand. But she does not, she only takes the work-basket and a book, and says good-night with an inclination of her little head.

I go over and stand next her chair ; I don't like to sit in it, but I like to put my hand where her head leant, and fancy, if she were there, how she would look up.

I woke next morning with a curious sense of pleasurable excitement. I whistled from very lightness of heart as I dressed. When I got down I found the landlady clearing away her breakfast things. I felt disappointed and resolved to be down earlier in future. I didn't feel inclined to try the minnow. I put them in a tub in the yard and tried to read and listen for her step. I dined alone. The day dragged terribly. I did not like to ask about her, I had a notion she might not like it. I spent the evening on the river. I might have filled a good basket, but I let the beggars rest. After all, I had caught fish enough to stock all the rivers in Great Britain. There are other things than trout in the world. I sit and smoke a pipe where she caught me last night. If I half close my eyes I can see hers, and her mouth in the smoke. That is one of the curious charms of baccy, it helps to reproduce brain pictures.

After a bit, I think 'perhaps she has left.' I get quite feverish at the thought and hasten back. I must ask. I look up at the window as I pass; there is surely a gleam of white. I throw down my traps and hasten up. She is leaning with her arms on the window-ledge staring out into the gloom. I could swear I caught a suppressed sob as I entered. I cough, and she turns quickly and bows slightly. A bonnet and gloves and lace affair and a lot of papers are lying on the table. I am awfully afraid she is going. I say—

'Please don't let me drive you away, it is so early yet. I half expected to see you on the river.'

'Nothing so pleasant; I have been up in town (the tears have certainly got into her voice) all day; it was so hot and dusty, I am tired out.'

The little servant brings in the lamp and a tray with a bottle of lemonade.

'Mistress hasn't any lemons, 'm, will this do?'

'Yes,' she says wearily, she is shading her eyes with her hand; 'anything; I am fearfully thirsty.'

'Let me concoct you a drink instead. I have lemons and ice and things. My man sent me down supplies to-day; I leave him in town. I am rather a dab at drinks; learnt it from the Yankees; about the only thing I did learn from them I care to remember. Susan!' The little maid helps me to get the materials, and *she* watches me quietly. When I give it to her she takes it with a smile (she *has* been crying). That is an ample thank-you. She looks quite old. Something more than tiredness called up those lines in her face.

* * * * *

Well, ten days passed, sometimes we met at breakfast, sometimes at supper, sometimes we fished together or sat in the straggling orchard and talked; she neither avoided me nor sought me. She is the most charming mixture of child and woman I ever met. She is a dual creature. Now I never met that in a man. When she is here without getting a letter in the morning or going to town, she seems like a girl. She runs about in her grey gown and little cap and laughs, and seems to throw off all thought like an irresponsible child. She is eager to fish, or pick gooseberries and eat them daintily, or sit under the trees and talk. But when she goes to town—I notice she always goes when she gets a lawyer's letter, there is no mistaking the envelope—she comes home tired and haggard-looking, an old woman of thirty-five. I wonder why. It takes her, even with her elasticity of temperament, nearly a day to get young again. I hate her to go to town; it is extraordinary how I miss her; I can't recall, when she is absent, her saying anything very wonderful, but she converses all the time. She has a gracious way of filling the place with herself, there is an entertaining quality in her very presence. We had one rainy afternoon; she tied me some flies (I shan't use any of them); I watched the lights in her hair as she moved, it is quite golden in some places, and she has a tiny mole near her left ear and another on her left wrist. On the eleventh day she got a letter but she didn't go to town, she stayed up in her room all day; twenty times I felt inclined to send her a line, but I had no excuse. I heard the landlady say as I passed the kitchen window: 'Poor dear! I'm sorry to lose her!' Lose her? I should think not. It has come to this with me that I don't care to face any future without her; and yet I know nothing about her, not even if she is a free woman. I shall find that out the next time I see her. In the evening I catch a glimpse of her gown in the orchard, and I follow her. We sit down near the river. Her left hand is lying gloveless next me in the grass.

'Do you think from what you have seen of me, that I would ask a question out of any mere impertinent curiosity?'

She starts. 'No, I do not!'

I take up her hand and touch the ring. 'Tell me, does this bind you to any one?'

I am conscious of a buzzing in my ears and a dancing blurr of water and sky and trees, as I wait (it seems to me an hour) for her reply. I felt the same sensation once before, when I got drawn into some rapids and had an awfully narrow shave, but of that another time.

The voice is shaking.

'I am not legally bound to any one, at least; but why do you ask?' she looks me square in the face as she speaks, with a touch of haughtiness I never saw in her before.

Perhaps the great relief I feel, the sense of joy at knowing she is free, speaks out of my face, for hers flushes and she drops her eyes, her lips tremble. I don't look at her again, but I can see her all the same. After a while she says—

'I half intended to tell you something about myself this evening, now I *must*. Let us go in. I shall come down to the sitting-room after your supper.' She takes a long look at the river and the inn, as if fixing the place in her memory; it strikes me with a chill that there is a good-bye in her gaze. Her eyes rest on me a moment as they come back, there is a sad look in their grey clearness. She swings her little grey gloves in her hand as we walk back. I can hear her walking up and down overhead; how tired she will be, and how slowly the time goes. I am standing at one side of the window when she enters; she stands at the other, leaning her head against the shutter with her hands clasped before her. I can hear my own heart beating, and, I fancy, hers through the stillness. The suspense is fearful. At length she says—

'You have been a long time out of England; you don't read the papers?'

'No.' A pause. I believe my heart is beating inside my head.

'You asked me if I was a free woman. I don't pretend to misunderstand why you asked me. I am not a beautiful woman, I never was. But there must be something about me, there is in some women, "essential femininity" perhaps, that appeals to all men. What I read in your eyes I have seen in many men's before, but before God I never tried to rouse it. To-day (with a sob), I can say I am free, yesterday morning I could not. Yesterday my husband gained his case and divorced me!' she closes her eyes and draws in her under-lip to stop its quivering. I want to take her in my arms, but I am afraid to.

'I did not ask you any more than if you were free!'

'No, but I am afraid you don't quite take in the meaning. I did not divorce my husband, he divorced *me*, he got a decree *nisi*; do you understand now? (she is speaking with difficulty), do you know what that implies?'

I can't stand her face any longer. I take her hands, they are icy cold, and hold them tightly.

'Yes, I know what it implies, that is, I know the legal and social conclusion to be drawn from it,—if that is what you mean. But I never asked you for that information. I have nothing to do with your past. You did not exist for me before the day we met on the river. I take you from that day and I ask you to marry me.'

I feel her tremble and her hands get suddenly warm. She turns her head and looks at me long and searchingly, then she says—

'Sit down, I want to say something!'

I obey, and she comes and stands next the chair. I can't help it, I reach up my arm, but she puts it gently down.

'No, you must listen without touching me, I shall go back to the window. I don't want to influence you a bit by any personal magnetism I possess. I want you to listen—I have told you he divorced me, the co-respondent was an old friend, a friend of my childhood, of my girlhood. He died just after the first application was made, luckily for me. He would have considered my honour before my happiness. *I* did not defend the case, it wasn't likely—ah, if you knew all? He proved his case; given clever counsel, willing witnesses to whom you make it worth while, and no defence, divorce is always attainable even in England. But remember: I figure as an adulteress in every English-speaking paper. If you buy last week's evening papers—do you remember the day I was in town?'—I nod—'you will see a sketch of me in that day's; some one, perhaps he, must have given it; it was from an old photograph. I bought one at Victoria as I came out; it is funny (with an hysterical laugh) to buy a caricature of one's own poor face at a news-stall. Yet in spite of that I have felt glad. The point for you is that I made no defence to the world, and (with a lifting of her head) I will make no apology, no explanation, no denial to you, now nor ever. I am very desolate and your attention came very warm to me, but I don't love you. Perhaps I could learn to (with a rush of colour), for what you have said to-night, and it is because of that I tell you to weigh what this means. Later, when your care for me will grow into habit, you may chafe at my past. It is from that I would save you.'

I hold out my hands and she comes and puts them aside and takes me by the beard and turns up my face and scans it earnestly. She must have been deceived a good deal. I let her do as she pleases, it is the wisest way with women, and it is good to have her touch me in that way. She seems satisfied. She stands leaning against the arm of the chair and says—

'I must learn first to think of myself as a free woman again, it almost seems wrong to-day to talk like this; can you understand that feel?'

I nod assent.

'Next time I must be sure, and you must be sure,' she lays her fingers on my mouth as I am about to protest, 'S-sh! You shall have a year to think. If you repeat then what you have said to-day, I shall give you your answer. You must not try to find me. I have money. If I am living, I will come here to you. If I am dead, you will be told of it. In the year between I shall look upon myself as belonging to you, and render an account if you wish of every hour. You will not be influenced by me in any way, and you will be able to reason it out calmly. If you think better of it, don't come.'

I feel there would be no use trying to move her, I simply kiss her hands and say:

'As you will, dear woman, I shall be here.'

We don't say any more; she sits down on a

footstool with her head against my knee, and I just smooth it. When the clocks strike ten through the house, she rises and I stand up. I see that she has been crying quietly, poor lonely little soul. I lift her off her feet and kiss her, and stammer out my sorrow at losing her, and she is gone. Next morning the little maid brought me an envelope from the lady, who left by the first train. It held a little grey glove; that is why I carry it always, and why I haunt the inn and never leave it for longer than a week; why I sit and dream in the old chair that has a ghost of her presence always; dream of the spring to come with the May-fly on the wing, and the young summer when midges dance, and the trout are growing fastidious; when she will come to me across the meadow grass, through the silver haze, as she did before; come with her grey eyes shining to exchange herself for her little grey glove.

AN EMPTY FRAME.

It was a simple pretty little frame, such as you may buy at any sale cheaply; its ribbed wood, aspinalled white, with an inner frame of pale blue plush; its one noticeable feature, that it was empty. And yet it stood on the middle of the bedroom mantel-board.

It was not a luxurious room, none of the furniture matched, it was a typical boarding-house bedroom.

Any one preserving the child habit of endowing inanimate objects with human attributes might fancy that the flickering flames of the fire took a pleasure in bringing into relief the bright bits in its dinginess. For they played over the silver-backed brushes, and the cut-glass perfume-bottles on the dressing-table; flicked the bright beads on the toes of coquettish small shoes and the steel clasps of a travelling bag in the corner; imparting a casual air of comfort, such as the touch of certain dainty women lends to a common room.

A woman enters, a woman wondrously soft and swift in all her movements. She seems to reach a place without your seeing how, no motion of elbow or knee betrays her. Her fingers glide swiftly down the buttons of her gown ; in a second she has freed herself from its ensheathing, garment after garment falls from her until she stands almost free. She gets into night-dress and loose woollen dressing-gown, and slips her naked feet into fur-lined slippers with a movement that is somehow the expression of an intense nervous relief from a thrall. Everything she does is done so swiftly that you see the result rather than the working out of each action.

She sinks into a chair before the fire, and, clasping her hands behind her head, peers into the glowing embers. The firelight, lower than her face, touches it cruelly ; picks out and accentuates as remorselessly as a rival woman the autographs past emotions have traced on its surface ; deepens the hollows of her delicate thoughtful temples and the double furrow between her clever irregular eyebrows. Her face is more characteristic than beautiful. Nine men would pass it, the tenth sell his immortal soul for it. The chin is strong, the curve of jaw determined ; there is a little full place under the chin s sharp point. The eyes tell you little ; they are keen and inquiring, and probe others' thoughts rather than reveal their own. The whole face is one of peculiar strength and self-reliance. The mouth is its contradiction—the passionate curve of the upper lip with its mobile corners, and the tender little under lip that shelters timidly beneath it, are encouraging promises against its strength.

The paleness of some strong feeling tinges her face, a slight trembling runs through her frame. Her inner soul-struggle is acting as a strong developing fluid upon a highly sensitised plate ; anger, scorn, pity, contempt chase one another like shadows across her face. Her eyes rest upon the empty frame, and the plain white space becomes alive to her. Her mind's eye fills it with a picture it once held in its dainty embrace. A rare head amongst the rarest heads of men, with its crest of hair tossed back from the great brow, its proud poise and the impress of grand confident compelling genius that reveals itself one scarce knows how ; with the brute possibility of an untamed, natural man lurking about the mouth and powerful throat. She feels the subduing smile of eyes that never failed to make her weak as a child under their gaze, and tame as a hungry bird. She stretches out her hands with a pitiful little movement, and then, remembering, lets them drop and locks them until the knuckles stand out whitely. She shuts her eyes, and one tear after the other starts from beneath her lids, trickles down her cheeks, and drops with a splash into her lap. She does not sob, only cries quietly, and she sees, as if she held the letter in her hand, the words that decided her fate—

'You love me; I know it, you other half of me. You want me to complete your life as I you, you good, sweet woman. You slight, weak thing, with your strong will and your grand, great heart. You witch with a soul of clean white fire. I kiss your hands (such little hands! I never saw the like), slim child-hands, with a touch as cool and as soft as a snow-flake! You dear one, come to me, I want you, now, always. Be with me, work with me, share with me, live with me, my equal as a creature; above me as my queen of women! I love you, I worship you, but you know my views. I cannot, I will not bind myself to you by any legal or religious tie. I must be free and unfettered to follow that which I believe right for me. If you come to me in all trust, I can and will give myself to you in all good faith, yours as much as you will, for ever! I will kneel to you. Why should I always desire to kneel to you? It is not that I stand in awe of you, or that I ever feel a need to kneel at all; but always to you, and to you alone. Come—I will crouch at your feet and swear myself to you,'—and she had replied 'No!' and in her loneliness of spirit married him who seemed to need her most out of those who admired her. . . .

The door opens and he comes in. He looks inquiringly at her, touches her hair half hesitatingly, and then stands with his hands thrust in his pockets and gnaws his moustache.

'Are you angry, little woman?'

'No' (very quietly), 'why should I be?'

She closes her eyes again, and after five minutes' silence he begins to undress. He does it very slowly, watching her perplexedly. When he has finished he stands with his back to the fire, an unlovely object in sleeping suit.

'Would you like to read her letter?'

She shakes her head.

'I suppose I ought to have sent her back her letters before, you know. She hadn't heard I was married.'

'Yes,' she interjects, 'it would have been better to start with a clean bill; but why talk about it?'

He looks at her a while, then gets into bed and watches her from behind the pages of the *Field*. It seems unusually quiet. His watch, that he has left in his waistcoat pocket, thrown across the back of a chair, seems to fill the whole room with a nervous tick.

He tosses the paper on to the floor. She looks up as it falls, rises, turns off the gas-jet, sinks back into her old position, and stares into the fire. He gets up, goes over, and kneels down next her.

'I am awfully sorry you are put out, old girl. I saw you were when I answered you like that, but I couldn't help feeling a bit cut up, you know. She wrote such an awfully nice letter, you know, wished'——

'you all sorts of happiness (with a snap) and hopes you'll meet in a better world?'

He rises to his feet and stares at her in dumb amazement. How could she know? She smiles with a touch of malicious satisfaction, as she sees the effect of her chance shot.

'It's a pity, isn't it, that you both have to wait so long?'

He imagines he sees light, and blunders ahead like an honest man.

'I wouldn't have sent those things back now if I had thought you cared. By Jove, it never entered my head that you'd be jealous!'

'Jealous? (she is on her feet like a red white flash). I, jealous of her? (each word is emphasised). I couldn't be jealous of her, *Nur die Dummen sind bescheiden!* Why, the girl isn't fit to tie my shoe-strings!'

This is too much; he feels he must protest.

'You don't know her (feebly). She is an awfully nice girl!'

'Nice girl! I don't doubt it, and she will be an awfully nice woman, and under each and every circumstance of life she will behave like an awfully nice person. Jealous! Do you think I cried because I was jealous? Good

God, no! I cried because I was sorry, fearfully sorry for myself. She' (with a fine thin contempt) 'would have suited you better than I. Jealous! no, only sorry. Sorry because any nice average girl of her type, who would model her frocks out of the *Lady's Pictorial*, gush over that dear Mr. Irving, paint milking-stools, try poker work, or any other fashionable fad, would have done for you just as well. And I' (with a catch of voice) 'with a great man might have made a great woman—and now those who know and understand me' (bitterly) 'think of me as a great failure.'

She finishes wearily, the fire dies out of eyes and voice. She adds half aloud as if to herself:

'I don't think I quite realised this until I saw how you took that letter. I was watching your face as you read it, and the fact that you could put her on the same level, that if it had not been for a mistake, she would have suited you as well, made me realise, don't you see? that I should have done better for some one else!'

He is looking at her in utter bewilderment, and she smiles as she notes his expression; she touches his cheek gently and leans her head against his arm.

'There, it 's all right, boy! Don't mind me, I have a bit of a complex nature; you couldn't understand me if you tried to; you'd better not try!'

She has slipped, whilst speaking, her warm bare foot out of her slipper, and is rubbing it gently over his chilled ones.

'You are cold, better go back to bed, I shall go too!'

She stands a moment quietly as he turns to obey, and then takes the frame, and kneeling down puts it gently into the hollowed red heart of the fire. It crackles crisply, and little tongues of flame shoot up, and she gets into bed by their light.

* * * * *

When the fire has burnt out, and he is sleeping like a child with his curly head on her breast, she falls asleep too and dreams that she is sitting on a fiery globe rolling away into space. That her head is wedged in a huge frame, the top of her head touches its top, the sides its sides, and it keeps growing larger and larger and her head with it, until she seems to be sitting inside her own head, and the inside is one vast hollow.

UNDER NORTHERN SKY

I

HOW MARIE LARSEN EXORCISED A DEMON

THERE has been a mighty storm, it has been raging for two days. A storm in which the demon of drink has reigned like a sinister god in the big white house, and the frightened women have cowered away, driven before the hot blast of the breath upon which curses danced, and the blaze of ire in the lurid eyes of the master. Only the pale little mistress has stood unmoved through the whirlwind of his passion. Who knows? Maybe that roused him to higher, madder paroxysms of impotent rage; for he abuses her most when he loves her most, a way man has, he being a creature of higher understanding.

All yesterday the bells jangled, until one by one a violent jerk snapped the connecting wire, and hurled them with a last echoing crash on the hall floor. The serving-men kept out of it as men do. The horses cowered to the sides of their boxes and set their hind legs hard, and pointed their ears when they heard his halting step. The great hounds shrunk shiveringly into their boxes, and refused to come forth to his threatening call ; and when he lashed their houses in his rage they winced at each blow, and showed their fangs when he turned away.

Night brought little rest, for lamps and candles were lit in every room ; champagne replaced brandy, then brandy champagne, and then both mingled in one glass. And in measure as the liquid fire was tossed down the poor parched throat, the brain grew clearer ; the intellect, with its Rabelaisque fertility of diseased imagining, keener ; the sting the tongue carried more adder-like, and the ingenuity of its blasphemies more devilish. The tired women crept to bed at midnight, to start in their sleep at the hoot of every night-owl, the flitter of every bat, and the whistle of every passing steamer ; all save the little mistress of the great house, with its stores of linen and silver ; its flower-filled garden ; its farmyard with lowing sleek kine ; its meadows in prime heart, heavy with the sweetness of red clover ;

its line of brown nets pegged down to catch the incoming eager salmon at the mouth of the fjord; and the wood with its peaceful nooks of cool green, and its winding paths with their brown carpet of last year's fir-needles and pine cones. She sits wearily in her low chair with her thin hands clasped on her sharp knees, and her shawl drawn round her shoulders, for in spite of the fire the first hour of the morning sends its chill breath into the room. He is lying on the sofa talking to himself, emphasising his words with his heavy stick. A table with decanters and glasses stands next him.

'Women, ay, women, man's curse. At the end of the race they beat us always. We get one soft spot with our mother's milk and well they know it, well they know it. What a man I would have been' (a rising growl) 'if it hadn't been for women! Do you hear, you white-faced spawn! Yes, I mean it. God! when I look back. But' (chuckling) 'I paid them out, the brutes!' And curse follows curse, and worse than that; as from the lips of the step-daughter in the fairy tale, the words that drop from his lips are the toads and vipers of filth.

'If one could forget. There was one, one long ago. I might have spared her, she pleaded hard against me. Why do I think of her to-night? it is years, years ago. Ah, but I was big and beautiful in those days! She, she was an innocent little thing. I fascinated her like a snake, and I can see her eyes. They were blue with long lashes. I *can see them now*, curse them! She and the child, jibbering idiots both! oh' (groan), 'curses on you for a devil to plague me thus! Keep away! I say, keep away! How the ghosts dance about the room! There is another one I had forgotten. Light more candles, more!' (a shriek) 'more! I say all round the room—make a damn wake of it.'

Mutter, mutter—a sordine epic of Hades. She closes her eyes. The stick whirls past her, striking a vase off a table near her; she gets up, hands it to him without a word; he hiccoughs and laughs, and then he heaves one sob and cries bitterly with the great tears gushing forth in jets. She picks up his handkerchief and puts it into his hand, and he looks at her with a piteous softening of his wild eyes, and he says quietly, hiccoughing all the while like a child tired after a fit of passion—for man in all his passions has a little of the inconsequent child, it is only woman who sins with clear seeing.

'I am a brute, I know it, but you don't know what it is to see the ghosts of sins stirring in a man's soul like maggots in a dead rat. And the children, that is the worst of all. O God, my poor little girls! What will become of them? Oh! Oh!'

'But you settled for them!' soothing with her weary voice. 'But you settled for them all right!'

'O yes, the money 's all right. O Lord, yes! I settled, I settled,' with the reiteration of drunken gravity, 'I settled that. But the mother was a brute, a heartless brute; and she was a lady too, ay, in her own right. And she never asked a word about them, not one word. It was I, I, poor disreputable brute, that put them to nurse; and I loathed her for it. Ah! if you women knew what a hold simple goodness has on us! I met her once, I had one at each hand; I used to go to see them. Oh, they don't know, they don't know, God forbid! And she lay back in her victoria and looked at us, curse her! She has children now, legitimate ones, and my little girls don't know I 'm alive.

Oh, my poor little girls! They are so pretty. Mind you bury that locket with me, don't open it. Yes, yes, I know, don't think I don't trust you,—only woman I ever trusted in the world. But I 'm afraid for them; curse this water in my eyes' (sob); 'don't you imagine I'm crying, I'm not! It 's whiskey, pure unadulterated' (hiccough) 'whiskey, but I can't help thinking of them. The others, ay, Lord! how many others? I don't care about them, I settled for them, *they weren't ladies*, they 'll get on well enough; but these, my pretty little ones. I 'm afraid for them, afraid for them. I, who spared no man's daughter, how can I tell if some brute won't hurt mine? Oh God, oh God, how can they be good with such a father and such a mother?'

He drinks as he speaks, and pours out in grief and rage a wild torrent of prayers and curses.

'Ay, verily, it 's reaping the whirlwind! How the faces crowd round! they always come with the grey morning light! women's faces, girls' faces, child-girls' faces, oh, damn you, hide me from them! Hold me tight and keep them away, put your arms right round me. You are clean—a clean little thing, they can't come through you.'

And she holds the throbbing head in her arms, and hides the wild eyes in her breast, and she feels as if there is a rustle of trailing skirts about her, and waving hair, and a feel of women. And then he tears himself out of her clasp, and she falls bruising herself sorely, and he throws over the table with a shatter of falling glass, and bounds up the stairs, snatching a riding-whip out of the hall. He beats its gold head into jagged shreds of glitter on the maids' door, and shouts to them to rise and come down. He 'll show them he is master in his own house. He has eaten nothing all day, no, nor for many days; down at once or he 'll know why, and cook—cook his dinner and light fires—yes, fires everywhere. What does he pay them for, lazy sluts, what does he keep house for? . . . And so, man, the master mind of creation, asserts his authority, and the maids troop down, heavy-eyed and stupid with sleep; and bake, and roast, and giggle hysterically under their breath; and tell stories of other masters they have served, and goings on; and grind fresh coffee beans, and have white bread, and lump sugar, and cold fowl, for there is no one to say them nay, and the larders are full of good things; and only the pale little mistress knows how near the grand place is drawing to bankruptcy.

Morning came, and the table was decked and the dinner served, and taken out again untasted; and another storm simmered all through the sunny forenoon to burst like a hurricane over the house at noon.

The kitchen is empty and the fire has gone out; a wreck of crockery shows where the storm raged worst. The girls flew before the thunder of voice and flash of whip; the Swedish gardener left his birthright of song untouched and followed them; he is skylarking with them now up in the great loft; they have pulled up the ladder, and are pelting one another with last year's hay. The cow-girl, a wench from Hittedal, lured the cattle and goats and long-legged, heifer calves deeper into the woods with her quaint Lokke song, calling:

> 'Come, sweet breath, come cowslip, come rich milk,
> Aa lukelei aa lura, lura, luralai!'

Only the housemaid, who is consumptive, and who stays for the little mistress' sake, her own days in the land being numbered, has taken her Bible up to the look-out in the wood, and laid it open on the stone table. She is crushing the Linnae as she kneels into a fragrant incense; rocking to and fro to the sombre rhythm of the last book of Ecclesiastes.

And the master of them all is sitting exhausted in his big chair, and Marie Larsen and he are doing battle. She came on the scene just as the grand retreat was sounded, and took the enemy by stratagem. She lifted the little mistress bodily up, and carried her up-stairs, leaving him, as she puts it, to ramp like a bull of Basan below. She lays her on her bed, takes off her shoes, pulls down the blind, and pours out some drops out of a little blue bottle she carries in her pocket, talking as she might to a child: 'There, Tulla, take naphtha drops, very good drops, you go sleep, good sleep, Marie mind him, Marie not afraid,' and with a final pat she goes down. He is laughing between his oaths at the stampede of petticoats, and he holds out his arms when she comes in.

She is a little square woman, between fifty and sixty, with a ruby button of a nose and hair, that oil and age has robbed of its brilliant red, drawn smoothly back into a tight screw at the back of her broad head. Her eyes are a fishy green grey, the left eyelid droops; when she thinks you are not looking, a sly elusive gleam brightens them, her pursed lips loosen, and if you happen to see it, you think that there may be something after all in the stories the gossips whisper of Marie Larsen. Her dress is exquisitely neat, her apron snowy. No one in the district can make such a *suprême* of fish as Marie; no one beat her at roasting a capercailzie and serving it with sour cream sauce; or brew such caudles and possets for a lying-in, or bake such meats for a funeral-feast. And what if there be an old-time tale of a brat accidentally smothered? And what if the Amtmanden (superior magistrate), he who had the sickly wife, did send Marie to Germany to learn cooking? Well, he had money to spare and was always freehanded. And if Nils Pettersen did write home and say that he saw her in Hamburg at a trade—well, other than cooking—sure Nils Pettersen was a bit of a liar anyhow, and good cooking covers a multitude of frailties. And if her nose was red and her breath smelt of cloves, who could say they ever saw her buy a bottle of akavit, and that was more than could be said of all the other temperance leaguers.

She had a nice cottage, with marigolds and curly-mint and none-so-prettys nodding down the garden paths, and if you went inside it was very respectable; and you could not fail to notice the large brass-bound Bible on a crochet-square on top of the mahogany chest of drawers, with a sprig of palm marking the gospel of the previous Sunday. And no one answered the responses more loudly, or confessed more openly at revival times, or quoted scripture more aptly to the confusion of a neighbour than Jomfru Marie Larsen. And then she had seen life too, and told them round the oven in winter over a cup of good coffee 'tales that were human,' just to warn them what risks they might run if they should be tempted to stray to the ungodly cities of the wicked world outside.

She stands and smiles at him.

'Arcades ambo! Blackguards both!' quotes he, pointing to a glass. She pours him out a measure and blinks, and fills a wine-glass with raw spirit for herself, and clinks glasses and sips like a connoisseur. And then she takes out her knitting and sets the needles flying. So they sit a while; his last grand charge has taxed him, but the quiet maddens him.

'Where's the Frue?' he asks, 'the Frue?'

She lays her head sideways on her hand and closes her eyes, saying in English: 'No can have Fruen, she sick, no can have her, be good, Marie tell you a tale.'

She gets up and shuts the doors; he roars at her and tries to rise, but his knees fail him; he sinks back into the chair and begins to swear. She knits away and commences in Norwegian a sing-song recitative like the drowsy buzz of a fly on a pane.

'Yesterday we had a bazaar, a bazaar in the school-house, a bazaar for the poor black heathens in Africa. For the poor black heathens lost in the darkness of unbelief, and ignorant of the saving of the Lamb—oh, it was a blessed work!'

A savage roar from him, but she goes on unheeding with her narrative.

'And there were tables with lots of things to be sold, and there were tables with refreshments, and there were wreaths and flags upon the walls, and godly texts and paper roses, yellow and red;' she draws out each word to spin the yarn longer, and he curses her for a Jezebel and foams with rage, and she sips her cognac with a deeper droop of eyelid and slower click of needle and proceeds with her tale:—

'And we had hymns, and the kapelan (curate) played the harmonium, and then he held a little edifying discourse, and the school children sang, and Marie had to hand round refreshments, and oh, it was a rousing day! And there was Frue[1] Magistrate Holmsen, and Frue Assessor Schwartz, and Frue Custom-house Chief's lady and her sister Fröken Dase, she of the long nose and pinched waist, and her engaged, the Candidat. And there was Frue Doctor Barthelsen, and Frue general dealer Steen and daughter, with a high frill to hide the evils in her neck, and Frue Insurance Agent. . . .' She dodges a glass adroitly, and raises her voice to drown his shriek of what the merry devil she means. 'Insurance Agent Hansen, and the Kaptein of the *Sea Gull*. . . . S-s-s, you be quiet, Marie tell you tale—there was Ma'm Sörensen and fat Ma'm Larsen; she's going to have her twelfth, and Larsen only

[1] The title Frue is properly borne by the wives of officials, but all the professional men's wives bear it. Madam is used by the small shopkeepers or lower burgher class, but the distinction is dying out. A Frue's daughter is Fröken, Madam's Jomfrue.

third mate, and Ma'm Johnsen and all the young gentlemen and ladies, and oh, it was a glorious sight!' She starts a key higher, for he is purple with fury and exertion, 'and, and we had coffee two pence a cup, and chocolade,' with a long-drawn stress on the 'lade' 'and Brus-selzers and lemonade and fruit juice and temperance beer. . . . No, no, you be quiet, Marie tell tale!'

He is struggling till the veins stand in cords to get out of his chair, but in vain; he points to his glass in desperation. She refills it and her own . . . 'Yes, temperance beer, a penny a glass, and we had white bread and brown bread and currant buns and Berlin kringels and ginger nuts and little cakes with hundreds and thousands on top! And oh, it was grand! . . .'

She is yelling louder and louder, and he is swearing deeper, and the battle shows no signs of ceasing.

'And then we sold all sorts of things, and drew numbers, and had a lucky bag; and Hans Jacobsen played on the melodeon, and missionary Hansen told us about the poor blacks, and all his blessed work, and how the Lord guided his footsteps through the sandy wastes, and how he baptized a chief and all his wives in the waters of faith. And Nils Pettersen says, they took out more raw alcohol and spent gunpowder and spoilt cotton goods than the fear of God; and that the *Bird o' Faith* cleared 100 per cent. on her freight. But Nils Pettersen was always a liar; and oh, it was a blessed thing to do all that for the heathen blacks! And then the kapelan spoke again, a touching discourse!' And she refills her glass, dodging his stick and watching him out of the tail of her eye as she turns the heel of her stocking, and repeats the whole of the sermon. His vocabulary is exhausted, and he is inventing the weirdest oaths, hurling them forth, a deep accompaniment to her shriller sermon, with its sanctimonious sing-song tune and unctuous phrasing; for she is, perhaps unwittingly, mimicking the kapelan to the life. He is getting tired and drowsy, the cognac is rising to her head, and even a kapelan's sermon must draw to a close. And as a mother will change her lullaby into a quick hushoo, and pat mechanically with a drowsy nod as the child drops to sleep, so Marie puts her knitting tidily into her apron pocket, and folding her withered old hands, breaks into a hymn. He opens his eyes languidly, and protests feebly with a last damn, but Marie has exorcised the devil this time. His jaw drops, and muttering softly, he falls into heavy sleep—and she sings on till her head too droops on her breast, and her quavering old woman's voice dies away in an abortive hallelujah!

And the motes dance in the golden bar of a waning sun ray that pierces the room and crosses the motionless figures—and above stairs the little mistress is wrapped in rare, delicious, dreamless slumber. And I like to think that the recording angel registered that sleep to the credit of Jomfrue Marie Larsen!

II.

A SHADOW'S SLANT.

IT is a sunny afternoon in mid-summer. A phaeton drawn by a pair of sturdy grey Stavanger horses, whose dainty heads and the mark of St. Olaf's thumb on their throats tell their race, is dashing along at a break-neck pace. The whip curls over them and the vehicle sways a little to one side. Two great hounds bound along on the right of it.

A strip of blue fjord and a background of dark mountains, with the cool ice-kisses of the snow queen still resting on their dusky heads, can be seen at intervals through the fir and pine trees. A squirrel scrambles up a rowan tree, and a cattle bell tingles far in the woods. Nature has ever a discordant note in its symphony. A little brown bird is fluttering in helpless terrified jerks; it emits, as it rises and falls, a sharp sound between a chirp and a squeak—a hawk is swooping over it—a poise—

a dip—a few feathers float with the breeze, and the hawk soars up with its prey in its claws.

The red-brown eyes that gleam out of the small sallow face of the woman who sits on the left side of the phaeton close for a second; the delicate nostrils quiver, the lips tighten over a sigh—then the lids rise again, the eyes are darker, the pupils have a trick of dilating; a smile subtle in meaning, for much of mocking pain and bitterness is expressed in its brief passage, flits across her face.

A savage jerk—the horses stop.

'Kiss me!' says the man who is driving, his voice is harsh and the eyes that scan her face have a lurid light in them, and as he speaks a smell of spirit mingles with the smell of the pine chips. Her lips tighten still more; she turns to obey. She has to rise up a little, he is very tall. His nose is powerful like a hawk's beak, and his beard is stirred by the breeze, and his eyes peer out from under their fringe of black lashes with a cruel passionate gleam. She almost touches his face but falls back from a rough shove—

'No, keep your kiss and be damned to you!'

A savage whoop, the whip curls out and the

reins jerk, and the quivering horses that know the voice too well dash on; and the hounds that have felt the whip-cord sting, as the strike of a snake on their flanks, bay savagely as they join in the race.

On the right of the narrow winding road a great lake lies hundreds of feet below; the wheel is not half a foot from the edge, and the vehicle jolts and leans that way, and the lash coils round and it flicks her ear, and leaves a sorry sting, and she never winces at it. But her small hands clench, and her lips part, and the red light flashes in her eyes, and something akin to exultant expectation steals over the thin small face as they court death, each wheel-turn in their mad career.

* * * * *

The stable door opens and the horses turn their heads. She, it is she, goes over and passes her fingers gently over the swollen stripes that make little ridges in the close-clipped hair. Once she lays her cheek caressingly upon a cruel furrow and whispers, 'Poor little Ola, if I had only governed my face better, you would not have been so punished;' and Ola turns his satiny muzzle, softer than the daintiest lady's breast, and rubs it against her, to coax for the apples that always follow. She goes from one to the other and coos to them and rubs her chin against their soft noses, and when the stripes are very bad her jaws set; and one can see the mark of the teeth through her thin cheeks.

* * * *

'Come here! I want some brandy! . . . . Now put the glass down and come back. What's that mark on your cheek?'

'Only the whip touched me.'

'And you were too damned proud to say so, eh? By the way, I saw some gipsies in the park. Johann can do the translating, they are coming here to play. One of them is a thundering fine girl, I'd like to . . . . what? what's that you said?'

'I did not make any remark!' a fine scorn trembles about her pale lips, and her face is a shade greyer.

A pause.

'Where are your rings?'

'Up-stairs!'

'Go and fetch them! Blast it! I don't buy you rings to leave them up-stairs.'

She comes back with them on, and he takes up the slim fingers laden with jewelled bands, spreads them out on his palm, then closes his thumb and finger round her wrist, and laughs a rasping laugh.

'Did any mortal man ever see such a hand? You witch! with eyes that probe into a fellow's soul and shame him and fear nothing!' and he tightens his grip and she winces at his roughness. 'There' (with a softening of voice), 'did I hurt you? you poor little thing, you queer little womany! Come closer' (with fierce, impatient tenderness); 'put down your little old head, a head like a snipe, on my breast. There, great God, I'm very fond of you!' a tremor runs through his voice. 'You queer little thing. You are no beauty, but you creep in, and I, I love every inch of you. I'd kiss the ground under your feet. I know every turn of your little body, the slope of your shoulders, I that always liked women to have square shoulders—the swing of your hips when you walk. Hips! ha, ha! you haven't got any, you scrap! and yet, by the Lord, I'd *lick* you like a dog' (slower, with emphasis), 'and *you* don't care for me. You obey me, no matter what I ask.' . . . .

He is holding her face against his breast, and stroking her head with clumsy touch. 'You wait on me, ay, no slave better, and yet—I can't get at you, near you; that little soul of yours is as free as if I hadn't bought you, as if I didn't own you, as if you were not my chattel, my thing to do what I please with; do you hear' (with fury) 'to degrade, to—to treat as *I please*? No, you are not afraid, you little white-faced thing, you obey because you are strong enough to endure, not because you fear me. And I know it, don't you think I don't see it. You pity me, great God! pity *me*—me that could whistle any woman to heel—yes, you pity me with all that great heart of yours because I am just a great, weak, helpless, drunken beast, a poor wreck!' and the tears jump out of his eyes, eyes that are limpid and blue and unspoiled; and he sobs out: 'Kiss me, take my head in your arms, I am a brute, an infernal brute, but I'm awfully fond of you, you queer little gipsy with your big heart and your damnable will. I! I! I who hated women like poison, who always treated them as such—I could cry when I look at you, like a great puling boy, because your spirit is out of my grasp. Smooth my head; no other little hand in the world has such a touch as yours. I'd know it amongst a thousand—my poor little thing! Don't ever leave me, promise even if I go mad, promise you'll stay. Get a man to mind me, but stay, won't you? Stay!'

'I'll stay.'

'Did any Christian man ever have such an atom for a wife? I believe you are a gipsy; your hair curls at the ends like a live thing, and there are red lights in its black, and your eyes have a flash in them at times and a look as if you were off in other lands! Oh, oh! Get me a little brandy, quick, quick!'

* * * * * *

Merrily twang the guitars, and the tambourines rattle as they are swung aloft by slender curving wrists. The wild cries of a Zingari dance ring out. Black eyes gleam, and brown skins shine under orange and scarlet kerchiefs. The grace of panthers and the charm of wild untamed natural things is revealed in every movement. Colour, vivacity, dirt, and rhythm.

Wild the music, wilder the dance, and he sits in his chair on the veranda, the clean, clear air and the fresh breeze blowing in from the sea, stirring the white hairs in the curls at his temples, and listens and looks with no eye or ear for aught of its beauty—only a ribald jest as their petticoats rise, or their bosoms quiver in the fling of the dance . . . . and she with a crimson shawl drawn round her spare shoulders, and a splash of colour in her thin cheeks holds one hand tightly pressed over her breast—to still what? What does the music rouse inside that frail frame, what parts her lips and causes her eyes to glisten and the thin nostrils to quiver? Is there aught in common between that slight figure with its jewelled hands and its too heavy silken gown, and those tattered healthy Zingari vagabonds? . . . . who knows?

The whole tribe are gathered round him, begging and screaming with one voice, and he throws silver lavishly to them and thrusts his hand with a coarse jest into the open bodice of the girl nearest him. A brown hand goes to the knife of a swarthy youth with gold rings in his ears; but at a few strange words from the oldest woman in the group the girl steps back, and with the quickness of lightning the hag takes her place and answers his jest in his own tongue. The girl looks curiously, pityingly, respectfully at the other girl, she is a little more than a girl as she stands dumbly by during all this scene. Eye seeks eye—sympathy meets sympathy—what affinity is between these two creatures?

'Kan de rokra Romany?' she asks with a smile that visits her face as the ghost of a vanished beauty; and her voice is sweetly soft as she asks it. A flash of eye, a hurried backward word thrown to the old woman who joins them on hearing it. She stands between with a smile at their wonder, and she holds out her hand, and one slim ivory-tinted hand rests palm upwards in a no less slim but browner one. The old woman peers into the lines and crosses, and as she scans them a look of wonder creeps up to her usually inscrutable face. She exchanges words in an undertone with the gipsy girl at her side.

'I speak Romany too, Deya! An evil fate, isn't it, mother?'

'A mole on your cheek, and a free Romany heart in your breast, your spirit fights to be free as the Romany chai. Seven suns rise and seven moons, and the flag is half-mast, and the cage opens and the bird . . . .' an impatient curse cuts short her words, and they turn to him.

'Here, you old Jezebel! Send these vagabonds of yours down there, there's plenty to eat.'

The servants are bearing beer and food to the lawn.

'Shall I go blind? I daresay you know as much as those infernal doctors, eh?'

'No, your eyes, and pretty eyes they are, and many a soul they've lost, they'll last your time, my lord! I see a journey to England, it lies before you, and no return. Seven times the moon will rise, and the Romanies go to the South, but the bird. . . .'

'Get to blazes out of this! Help me in, ducky, oh damn it, be quick. Get me some brandy, quick, quick,—not all brandy, a little milk in it!'

* * * * * *

The moon is high in the heavens, and the sea is running into the creek with a silver sheen on its back; the blinds are drawn up in the four windows of the bedroom, and the northern night is like unto day disguised in a domino of silver-grey crape.

He is sleeping. She is standing motionless at the window. The red of her dressing-gown and the moonlight make her face look more ghostlike as she leans her head wearily against the window-frame. She is gazing seawards; a steamer has just passed, and the beacon in the lighthouse on Jomfru-land gleams like a great bright eye. In how many dreary vigils has it not greeted her and seemed to say: 'Courage, I too am watching, you are not alone.'

At the end of the wood two tents are pitched, and she can see two figures outlined against the white palings. The Romany girl and the youth with the gold ear-rings. He is holding her in his arms. The dog-chains rattle now and then; something brown and stealthy creeps about the duck-house; the white mists in the marshy bit of meadow lying next the creek dance like spirits, and beckon to her with shadowy arms, and a faint yellow streak appears in the East. How many more nights must she stand alone and watch the morning herald a new day of bondage? She moves noiselessly away, and goes into the dressing-room, and walks over to the mirror. She shakes her dusky elf locks round her face, and catching up a yellow scarf lying on a chair, winds it round her head, and then peers at herself in the glass. . . . A deft twist turns down the white frills of her night-gown, she has a gold chain round her neck, and she laughs a childish noiseless laugh at her own image. 'How strangely my eyes gleam, and what a gipsy I look! No one would know, no one would dream of it. I would soon get brown!' and she looks wistfully out towards the camp again. In an hour they will go . . . a heap of fern to lie on, scant fare, and weary feet; but the freedom, ah, the freedom! The woods with their wealth of shy, wild things, and the mountains that make one yearn to soar up over their heights to the worlds above. Free to follow the beck of one's spirit, a-ah to dream of it, and the red light glows in her eyes again; they have an inward look; what visions do they see? The small thin face is transformed, the lips are softer, one quick emotion chases the other across it, the eyes glisten and darken deeply, and the copper threads shine in her swart hair. What is she going to do, what resolve is she making? A muttered groan, a stir in the bed rouses her, and throwing aside the scarf, she glides swiftly to his side. She stands and looks down. What a magnificent head it is, and how repellent! The tossed black locks with their silver streaks lie scattered on the pillow. The ear suggests vigorous animalism, the nose is powerful, the broad forehead shines whitely, and the long lashes curl upward as those of a child. The sensual-lipped mouth with its cruel lines shows more cruel as the head is thrown back. She looks at it steadily, no line escapes her; looks from it to the hands, nerveless, white. The long thin thumbs have a hateful expression, and the backs are short with an ugly joining to the wrists. He stirs, and a lewd word escapes his lips. . . . She shudders. Again her eyes wander out with an appealing look (to whom do they appeal, to part of herself, to some God of convention?) towards the camp. They are stirring, she can see the Finn dog run to and fro. She steps away . . . irresolution is expressed in her face, her head is thrust forward, her fingers spread out unconsciously. . . . She glances across the floor, some shelves are to be nailed up, one of them is leant against the wardrobe door. As she hesitates she notices that the shadow of it and the half-closed door throws a long cross almost to her feet. She folds her hands involuntarily —a whimper from the bed, a frightened call—

'Come to me! Where are you? Don't leave me a second, oh God, don't leave me! What's that there? Give me a drop of brandy, quick, oh quick! . . . Kneel down, dearie, close, close to me, lay your little old cheek against mine, and say a little prayer, no psalm business, just one out of your own little head' (sob) 'to suit a poor devil like me!'

* * * * *

The sun is saying good-morning to the moon. She is wan from watching. The birds are awake, but the man still sleeps; and the little red-gowned figure crouched at the bed-side, her left hand with its heavy gold band clasped lightly in his, is sleeping too. A half-dried tear is held in the dark hollow under the closed eyes. The nose looks pinched in the morning light, and a grey-green shadow stains mouth and chin, but a smile plays round the dry lips.

The caravan is winding slowly round the curve of the road, and three plump geese are stowed inside. The Romany lass is humming a song, a song about love, and dance, and song; and the soul of the sleeping girl floats along at her side in a dream of freedom. She of the song looks up: 'Six moons will rise, then you will be free!' she mutters to herself as she passes on; and the sun mounts higher, and the shadow of the cross is lightening with the coming dawn —who knows?

III.

AN EBB TIDE

On right and left with flight of light,
How whirled the hills, the trees, the bowers!
With light-like flight, on left and right,
How spun the hamlets, towns, and towers!
Dost quail? The moon is fair to see;
Hurrah! the Dead ride recklessly!
Beloved! Dost dread the shrouded dead?
Ah let the dead repose! she said.'

James Clarence Mangan's *Anthology.*

It is a sunshine Sabbath morning. The sea quivers under an armour of silver scales and laps, laps with a laugh as it runs into the creek. The sails of the ships glisten whiter than any snow. The sun distils the scent from the clove carnations and the sweetbrier leaves; and coaxes the pungent resin through the cracks in the bark, until the air is heavy with a smell that would cease to be perfume, were it not filtered through the salt ooze of the incoming sea-breeze that flutters the flags on the tall white poles, and tempers the ardour of the young year's sun.

The kariol bearing the specialist whose skill

is of no avail in the face of a pressing call from the great God Death, has just wound round the pine wood in a whirl of dust. The dogs, unbound, lie on the back veranda with their black snouts resting on their fore paws, and they watch him depart without a growl. They have not barked for days past, nor chased the plucky badger, nor yapped impatiently as the cheeky squirrels flirted through the branches. Even beggars have come and gone without a snarling protest. But all last night they howled and bayed and cowered together as if they could see the passage of invisible guests. A peculiar stillness seems to brood over the great place. The maids are sitting in their gowns of Sunday black, with open psalm-books on their laps; they are listening and whispering with the disturbance of expectancy.

The housekeeper is talking to the leech woman, quaint survival of older days, whose business in life is to keep the slimy suckers lively and apply them. She looks as if she fed them between-times on herself, so bony and colourless a creature is she. They are negotiating the last ghastly offices that may soon be needed—speculating as to the changes and their effect on the village. Thc vicar, she tells, is about to make the departing life the text of his sermon. Every one in the district is coming to hear it. Why not? A sermon of warning, with a smack of the Pharisee in it, a 'Lord, I thank Thee I am not like unto this man' note, especially if you know the publican in question, cannot fail to be attractive; it has an up-to-date interest that the parable of the far-away-time sinner necessarily lacks.

Up-stairs the cow-girl is crouching like a faithful dog outside his bedroom door; she is listening to the murmured Latin service of the mass that comes from inside. The windows of the room are wide open, and the sea stretches away and melts into the horizon in an infinity of blue and silver. He is lying still on the ebb of his last tide, and when his eyes open they wander from the little priest before the extemporised altar, to the bowed head of the woman kneeling beside him.

'Pax Domini sit semper vobiscum!' intones the priest.

'Et cum spiritu tuo!' she utters in response, in dead, dull tones, and when she chimes the little silver bell she does it in a mechanical way.

And all the time he holds her one hand to his breast. When the mass is read and the extreme unction administered, the little priest reads the prayers for the dying. He listens attentively, and she listens too, with eyes dry as horn, and tightened lips. She scarcely hears what he reads.

'My feet have gone astray in the paths of vanity and sin, now let me walk in the way of Thy commandments. . . . Forgive me, O Lord, all the sins which I have committed by my disordered steps. . . .' 'Steps!' that means feet, 'eyes seen vanities,' that means sight. . . . 'Tongue hath in many ways offended,' speech; why he is going through all the seven senses, or is it seven? or five? She must give him the envelope with the cheque in it before he leaves. . . . She hasn't a black frock, not one; he liked her in colours, light girlish colours with a silken waist-band to match. Must she wire for a coffin? What a beast she is to think like this? But how can she help it? Her tear-bags—what is their right name? lachrymal glands?—are exhausted, even her lashes have thinned, yet she never shed a tear, at least only inwardly, with a choke.

He sobs and she looks up; the tears are trickling down his cheeks, she puts up her free hand and wipes them off gently.

'To Thee I resign my heart! Into Thy hands, O Lord, I commend my spirit!' reads the priest in broken English, and when the, from its point of view, beautiful prayer has drawn to a solemn close, the man sobs out in genuine heartfelt conviction with a force of epithet that is habit, not irreverence.

'That is a damn nice prayer! I was always afraid of death, always (with a sob) a coward, but when it comes to the point that vanishes too!'

And the boyish priest purses his cheque, and takes it with him, and leaves his blessing instead, and follows in the wake of the town doctor.

'Send Johann to me, dearums, let me get dressed, I'll have a try to die in the sunshine. Get your own little bed carried down to the veranda, and your own little white pillow; mind, the one you put your head on last; and lend them to me for this turn.'

And so the maids take it down, and she stands at the head of the stairs as they carry it, two at the head, and two at the foot. As she hears their cautious backward steps and the rest at the turn, she fancies it sounds like the bearing out of a coffin. And then he follows slowly out, leaning on his big stick, and his beard divides into patches and shows the purplish skin, and his breathing is laboured, but he steps more firmly than he has done for a long time past. He leans on her frail shoulders, and when they reach the dining-room he calls in the maids and the men who serve him, and bids them charge their glasses; and he thanks them, and says he is sorry for all the trouble he has given them, and shakes hands with each one; and they courtesy and say Skaal! (a salutation when drinking) and troop out crying. They are mostly women, and women forgive easily and forget everything—to a man! Only the cow-girl stops behind crouched near the door crying: 'O-ah, o-ah!' He fills his own glass with champagne and sips it, but nature sets a limit to the alcohol a man may absorb, and he has passed it. He cannot get it down, so he lays his hand on her head and smooths it gently, and says—

'Your luck, little one, your very good luck! Oh, my poor little one, I am afraid for you! I ought to have . . . well, it's no good regretting . . . and with a last flame of the old fierce fire he cries—

'I have had my last drink, and no man shall drink after me;' and he shivers the glass against the wall, and purple shadows, the 'skreigh' of another dawn, chase one another over his swollen face, and he leans heavily on her and says faintly—

'Lay me down, I am tired!'

'When they reach the veranda, the leaves of the virgin-vine are strewn in dancing shadow leaves and fluttering tendrils at their feet. He looks at them and mutters: 'Shadows—only shadows!'

Suddenly he searches her face intently and asks—

'Is there no hope, little one? none?'

He reads the answer in her wistful eyes.

'When? Don't you be afraid to tell me, when did he say?'

'Inside twenty-four hours—'

There is a long silence, and the shadow leaves dance, and the bees whirl buzzing past, and the strong young life of midsummer mocks dissolution in a subtle arrogant way.

'One good clean year, one clean year, one year's home for a finish. Just as I learnt to know what it meant to leave it all! It's hard to look on a day like this' (sob) 'and know that to-morrow I rot. A long life as lives go, and nothing to show for it. Well, I always wanted to die in the sunshine with the birds singing, and, since I knew you, with you near me—oh, my dear, my poor dear little one!'

He reels, and she clutches him, but he steadies himself by a supreme effort, and says through his ground teeth—

'Now I am going to say good-bye to the world, and, by God, I'll say it standing. I have had good days in it, wild, glad days, drunk with the lust of love and wine, but I never saw good or beauty in it till you showed me how. Oh, oh, oh! Let no man write my epitaph!'

He stands leaning on her shoulders looking seawards, drinking his fill of sun and sea, sea that was a rapture to him, that he loved as the greatest, and strongest, and cruellest thing he knew; the only thing that responded to the wild moods in his soul, and struck a rushing strain of song in his stormy heart, that made him rejoice with a fierce delight. The tears fall and splash on her hands, and then she helps him to lie down, and she feels his feet, and they bring hot bottles, for they are getting cold, and he lies with his eyes closed; the village doctor comes and goes, but nothing can be done, the sands are running out fast. 'If the Lord be merciful' (the sermon is working in him) 'He will take him before morning, otherwise he will suffer much,' he whispers to her. She does not answer, only kneels silently at his side, and he holds her hand. There is a strange smell that has a chill uncleanness in its breath about them. The people pass by on the road above and peer down through the palings. The maids give audience to inquisitive or interested callers at the back. The housekeeper is busy at the linen press, sorting out sheets and things that may be needed, and as she moves about with noiseless tread, and folds and lays aside, she mentally remodels her wardrobe. If she take out the flower in her black summer hat, and put in some curled tips, it will serve nicely. Mistress will surely bring her a dress from England, and the merino they hang the rooms with, she will get it cut the proper lengths, will do for the maids. Uf! that nasty wine gave her a headache! she will get some fresh beans roasted, and have a good cup with fresh cream; that will do her good. How Gudrun (the cow-girl) takes on! He was a devil to serve, but there were advantages, ay, many pickings that would not fall to one's share in better-regulated Christian households, not to speak of the distinct comfort of having a mistress whose time is taken up elsewhere. Poor thing! Well, it's best for her, she has money, she'll marry again. But *that* Gudrun! it is odd. Why should she carry on so? Or could there be a reason? He always took great notice of Gudrun; she used to laugh and grin and go on, when he went out in the yard, and never was afraid. And then there was that anonymous letter the mistress got. Uf! Men folk, God save us! Even with a leg in the grave it's hard to trust them! There's no smoke without fire, that's sure. There, that's all ready. 'Well! what is it?'

This to the second housemaid. She is a fat girl, with a restless twitch about her mouth and half-closed eye-lids, that curl upwards at the outer corners. One gets the impression somehow that her solid physique is but a mask to cover an emotional soul with a dangerous sense of humour.

'The Bible reader, Morten Ring, wants to know if he may read for a while, now that the Popish priest has gone and left the dying sinner without any one to direct his thoughts heavenwards.'

There is an imitative note in her voice, and a mocking gleam shoots from her eyes.

'Uf! is he here again? That's the third time. Mistress told him no before, and strong enough too; I should think that ought to have been more than enough for him.'

'Yes, but he says the whole village thinks it shocking and he is like sent up, and that you might put it to her!'

'Indeed, then I won't. When I did last time she told me to tell him to go down to the weighing place on the wharf, and ring a bell, and call the population together and read out to them all the places in the Bible that refer to hypocrisy, lying, and scandal; the sins of adultery, fornication, and the begetting of bastards. That she'd be willing to pay him treble his fee for the charity of it; they need it so much. It might teach them to begin at home and let other folks alone.'

'Shall I tell him that?' (eagerly.)

'Are you mad? No, tell him Mistress is reading herself, and ask him to stay and have a good cup of coffee and sweet rusks. I want to get the truth out of him about the magistrate's girl's illness; he was up there, and I don't believe a sniff in her sprained foot. . . .'

And down below the rosebuds opened into roses, and nodded with the effrontery of assured beauty to the Sun God; and the birds hushed them for their noon siesta; and he lay with shut eyes and held her hand tightly; and sometimes he spoke to her and sometimes he muttered to himself (she caught the words) a line of his favourite Mangan:

> 'Sleep! no more the dupe of hopes and schemes,
> Soon thou sleepest where the thistles blow;
> Curious anticlimax to thy dreams,
> Twenty golden years ago!'

The odd unpleasant smell seems to hang about

them as if too heavy to diffuse itself in the thin clear air; the smell of cow-sheds that clings to the cow-girl's clothes, is perfume to it. It attracted the flies and they gathered like swarming bees on the window panes and door posts; and buzzed and hummed and stung like Bushmen, carousing over a find of dead meat; and they crept over the bed and stuck in his hair, and she tried to keep them off his face, and when one of them crawled up her own with tickling, clinging feet, she paled and shuddered. The cow-girl stepped out of her clogs and went into the drawing-room and brought out a gaily-painted palm-leaf fan and stationing herself at the head of the bed, set it in motion. His breathing is getting laboured, and at times an ugly flush crosses his face. Once when it is deeper than usual, the girl cries: 'O Lord God, Lord God!' He hears her and looks up.

'Ah, Gudrun, is that you? good girl, good girl!'

She sinks on to her knees and moans and rocks herself, and then she looks at his closed eyes and says to her—

'Mistress, may I? It can't harm you!'

She nods her head wearily; she is fanning awkwardly with her left hand, and she says with her tired tender voice—

'Gudrun wants to say good-bye, dear!'

He opens his eyes, and for a moment the charm of his rare smile returns. The girl stoops and leaves a kiss upon his forehead, and then rushes away and flings herself down on the long lush grass, that is never cut, under a big chestnut tree. He looks at her and lifts her hand to his lips—

'Always a big heart, always a great little woman!' (with a groan) 'and now I am to lose you, and it is the best thing could happen to you. Ay, there 's the sting; leave you to some brute; that is my punishment. O little one, don't you think too hardly of me (he talks with effort), I meant to be better than I was to you. You 'll never find another man love you as I did; remember that and forget all the rest if you can. You *have* forgotten all, I might have known you would . . . where am I drifting to? no man ever came back to say. Do you believe in hell' (eagerly), 'do *you* believe in it?'

She looks at him pityingly, with a flash of past

energy in the lift of her head and a curl of scorn on her pale lips.

'The hell of the priests or parson? No, I do not. Is that worrying you? Don't you let it, old man, don't you let it. Wherever you are going, whatever after-existence your poor troubled soul is fighting its way to, it *is not to their hell.*' The girl has come back and taken up her former position, and fans steadily, for the flies are gathering in greater numbers every hour. The veranda seems airless and close, and uncanny with unseen things; the doctor comes and goes; the servants peep out; and the hours seem to hold many hours in their embrace. She seems to live all her life over again. Things she has forgotten completely come vividly back to her. An old Maori man, who used to sell sweet potatoes, and quaint ring shells for napkin rings to the Pakeha lady in Tauranga Bay, floats before her inward vision as tangible as if he were next her. And a soldier servant; she can hear his voice; he used to sing as he pipe-clayed—

'But kaipoi te waipero, Kaipoi te waiena
For Rangatira Sal, Bob Walker sold his pal,
But he 's now at the bottom o' the harbour.

Why did the stupid chorus come back to her now, what chink of brain did it lie in all these years? Oh what a brute she is and how callous! She ought to read prayers, or say things; in a few hours it will be too late to ever say a word more. She finds herself beating time with her foot to a jig tune, a bizarre accompaniment to the words 'too late.' She would give all she possesses to cry, yet she cannot; and so the day wears on.

Later on she bends her head to him and asks:

'Are you dozing or are you thinking? What are you thinking of?'

He smiles. 'Of zoo, dearums, of zoo!'

'Have you said your prayers; shall I read you any?'

'Finished them long ago! I am just waiting, lying thinking of you, dearie, thinking of you. Happier than ever I was since I left off "taw in the lay" and pegging tops.'

Her question was a concession to a past religious conscience; she feels as she puts it that as for herself if she should die as she sits there, she would not trouble to pray—it would be well to drift out. There is another weary hour's silence, then he looks up at her and shivers slightly, and tightens his clasp of her hand.

'Kiss me, duckums, kiss me! Now lay your little old phiz on the pillow close to mine, you dearest and best in the world! Close, close to mine.'

The wind is changing, and the sun hides his face decently behind a great white cloud; there is a hoarse rattle in his throat, and his breathing is difficult. The doctor comes and stands quietly behind her; the crowd at the gate above gets denser; the servants huddle together in the dining-room and cry. The Swedish gardener pats them all in turn, but most gently the fat housemaid. A sudden blast of wind blows a strand of her hair loose and it touches his lips, and he mutters, 'My little one!' She lifts her face and looks at him, a strange purple colour vibration is waving over his face, and she calls affrightedly—

'Dear, oh dear man, look at me! Can you see me, do you know me?'

He lifts his heavy lids and looks at her steadily with half-dead eyes, and says with stiff, barely articulate speech—

'Of course I do, my dearie, I'm all rig . . .!'

She feels his fingers close more tightly over hers—once—twice, then relax. His chin falls, and the doctor passes his hand over his eyelids and puts a handkerchief to his lips. The cow-girl drops with a cry to the ground and throws her apron over her head. At the gate above a child calls 'mammy' in frightened tones. The lad who has been sitting up on the slope at the foot of the flag-staff, slides the Union Jack half-mast, and the big white house is without a master.

* * * * * *

She is sitting in an old garden, a retired place in the village, right on the fjord. They have driven her down there away from the house that seems haunted by his spirit; infected with the loathsome odour of rapid dissolution that nothing can overcome, that seems to ooze out and taint the very flowers. And then the myriad flies that crawl and creep, as if sick or drunk, over everything; and make one loathe and turn from the very sight of food and drink, for dread of where they have been; make one long to scream hysterically to drown their hateful buzzing; and rush away and plunge into the sea—were it not that it too seems to whisper in undertones of dead men and lost sweethearts, drowned mariners with swollen grey-green faces and tangled locks floating like sea sedge behind them, as they toss on the swift undercurrents beneath its treacherous smiling surface.

It is with her, sitting there, as it is with most of us when numbed in mind and heart by some great trouble; her senses are more alive to outward sounds and scenes. It is as if when one's inner self is working with some emotion, wrestling with some potential moral enemy, crying out under the crucifixion of some soul-passion—eyes and ears and above all sense of smell are busy receiving impressions, and storing them up as a phonograph records a sound, to reproduce them with absolute fidelity if any of the senses be touched in the same way by the subtle connection between perfume and memory. She will, in all time to come, never forget that old garden. She is rocking unconsciously to and fro. Her thoughts, and the emotions belonging to them, cross one another rapidly; flash past as the landscape seen from a mail train, so that she cannot fasten any of them. The weary vigils of many months, the details of days and hours are ticked off as the events on a tape. The look in his eyes, press of his fingers, the quiet face with the awful look of peace—the rapid changes to a thing to be hidden away as swiftly as hands can coffin it; the clasped fingers never to be lifted in tender caress or angry gesture; the future to face without even the rough protection of his passionate wayward affection—all these conflicting images and reasonings dash through her brain and yet not a detail of her surroundings escapes her. The strips of blue fjord with the pilot boats with their numbered sails in the immediate foreground; and the prams, turned bottom up on the miniature wharf for a fresh coat of paint. The dip of the white sail of a pleasure-boat in the distance, and the gleam of the scarlet cap of a girl steering. Bright flecks on the black-green shadows of the trees in the near background, that stand out distinctly from the misty blue of the distant mountains; misty with the purple light that only clothes the northern heights. Not a detail of the quaint garden escapes her. It is a garden of surprises. Fruit-trees from strange lands, dwarf shrubs of foreign birth, curious shells gathered on the beach of far-away islands flourish promiscuously with indigenous plants. A painted lady (the figure-head of some effete sailing craft), who has cloven the storms through many seas with her mighty breasts, and commanded the rising waves with her upraised hand, and faced the storm with a smile ghastly in its wooden fixity, has come here to rest. She leans next to an old sun-dial in the shade of an ancient lilac bush. The sense of beauty, and the bump of utility of successive owners is manifested at every turn. The even drills of potatoes are disturbed by the tombstone of a favourite dog. A plaster Mercury, and a shrub, cut in the form of a bulgy tea-pot, spoil the symmetry of a bed of carrots. Strawberries carrying their ripe red fruit right bravely fill the background of one bed. A tangled profusion of pinks, pansies, and gillyflowers, forget-me-nots, and fragrant lavender spikes have a long straight line of leeks running amidst their sweet irregularity as a pungent line in a dainty sheaf of verse. She is conscious of a vague pleasure as she notes these things, and a sort of wondering pity at the pathos of her own quiet figure. She fingers her black cashmere gown and the heavy silk fringe of her shawl. She never wore a shawl before, but they had nothing else black. Her mother used to wear a shawl, a white Indian silk with raised flowers. Her shoulders sloped too, like Eugénie's. Funny to wear a shawl like an old lady! She has a bag with money, papers, certificate of death for the customs. What a nuisance all these formalities are! Lum tum, te tum, te tum . . .! The dead march in Saul! No, she mustn't hum that. She remembers once in the long ago, before the flood, her flood, she had a sweetheart, a boy officer. She wonders did he get fat; they always chaffed and said he would. Once she was humming it and he stopped her, saying: 'Oh don't! when any one hums that, a poor soldier dies somewhere.' Superstition of course, but she won't hum it all the same, just for the old sake's sake. Why should she kill a soldier? She used to like all soldiers, tum tum! . . . Is she going mad? How does one go mad? . . . She turns her head in relief at an approaching step. The little doctor stands bowing, hat in hand. She notices that he is wearing his dress suit, and adds mentally, 'they wear dress clothes on solemn occasions; christenings, weddings, funerals.' Why, of course it's the funeral! She even smiles at the conjunction of a swallow-tail with elastic side leather boots with high heels. His trousers too must have been made before he grew stout; they ruck up at the knees, and show the end line of his under-drawers quite plainly. She feels inclined to laugh. She hasn't really laughed for a long time; well, why shouldn't she laugh?

'Will Fruen come now?' he queries. There is a subtle blending of the soothing professional tone he uses to lady patients, and the gravity befitting a solemn occasion. She takes up her bag, gathers her shawl mechanically into graceful folds over her arms and follows him. They go up through the wood past the poorhouse to a side entrance. She notices as she looks down over the town that the flags are all half-way down the staffs, and that the village is crowded with folk; and that outside the house there are groups of black-coated men; like ants crawling about a white stone, she thinks. The little housekeeper meets her at the door; the other girls are crying; she bows to people without recognising them. Then there is a tramping of feet, and some one leads her out; the bell is tolling up from the church, and she sees that they have covered the grey cobs with black palls, and attached a black canopy to the cart, and outlined the spokes of the wheels with fir needles, and smothered the rest of it with branches and flowers, wreaths and crosses, and harps and lyres; he hated music too. The coffin—what an ugly black thing, with an exaggerated stomach and garish silver ornaments!—is resting upon the Union Jack. A crowd of faces that she does not know meets her. She places herself behind the cart, and the maids follow her, and all the dogs gather round her but never growl once as they move on, and the crowd follows. She can see the green road; they have covered it according to custom with branches of fir and pine, a green river, a grass-green river winding to the left. And the sea, the sea he loved! it seems to her that there is a cadence of pity in the eternal note of its quiet sadness. How tired her feet are; it 's quite half a mile yet; she has no ankles; how funny! Just stilts made of her will. She trips. The cow-girl pushes past the housekeeper, and watches her steps. 'Lord God, how stony-faced she is!' whispers the doctor's wife, 'and she never cried once.' It is a long way, she keeps thinking.

Where are they going anyway? Oh yes, to the tug, the tug that is to bear them away on a glorious lonely death-ride, out of the sunny fjord to the glistening sea, away to where the rainbow ends. At the end of the rainbow you 'll find a pot of gold. But first they must pass through the wide wooden gate; it is open. What is that they say about a wide wooden gate? No, it 's about a road, it 's the wide road that leads to destruction. They have decked the gate with green too. The gate through which the children used to peer with inquisitive frightened child-eyes, up to the house where the wicked man dwelt. How they used to scamper away with half-real, half-acted terror at a cry of, 'the man is coming!' the man who was a bogie-man to them, a name with which to threaten them when naughty; about whom their elders told dreadful tales in subdued voices. She remembers this, and smiles half sadly to see as they reach the narrow street how the children swarm to meet his coming. There is no school to-day, and they get under the horses' hoofs, and crowd round the car, and point with dirty chubby fore-fingers, and clasp hands and cluster together in groups of twos and threes, and gaze with awe-struck eyes, and whisper, and follow. And one whispers to his comrades how he once got a drive and a silver piece from 'the man,' and another how he gave little Tulla a piece of cake. And she thinks of the train that danced in the wake of the pied piper, and of his own little ones who know him not. Perhaps they are dancing and laughing to-day. To-day, when the father who gave them no name is being borne along to the tuneful patter of little feet that are not of his kith nor his kin. She seems to feel that that thing in the coffin is not he. He is walking next her, laughing with the rare humour of his best moments; chuckling at the grand funeral they are giving him; him the bad man, of whom they had naught but evil to say. How hard it is to go down hill slowly! She tells herself that later on in the ages to come, when the little ones here have gone to their last homes as withered elders, the tales of the bogie-man of their child days may have grown into a saga of a wild Angle-man with great wealth, who landed and made himself a home on their coast, and drank and caroused and bought the strangest things; who took mad sails in a boat right into the teeth of coming gales that the pilots feared to brave, when the white-crested horses leaped high over the rocks, and the sea dragons roared below, and the grey mews shrieked shrill warnings to the fishers to hasten them home. Who turned the night into day and took wild hag-rides with his baying and galloping horses at midnight, and how he used to crack his whip and urge them on with exultant oaths; and never let his little wife out of his sight, but called for her if he missed her till the woods rang with her name.

They reach the wharf, the tug *Bully-boy*, with black funnel and hissing steam is lying taut to the pier. Her head is really spinning. How stupid those eight men are! they haven't backed the horses enough. Hats off! They lay him on the deck, they have put the old flag under him and piled the posies on top. She pats the dogs and bids them stay, and lets the women kiss her, and walks up the plank; one plank, surely there should be four—

'For thee it is that I dree such pain
As when wounded even a plank will,
My bosom is pierced, is rent in twain,
That thine may ever bide tranquil.
    May ever remain
Henceforward untroubled and tranquil.'

No, that's not the verse, she can't get it.

'I heard four planks fall down with a saddening echo? . . . with a hollow echo?' She stands by the side of the coffin and gazes quietly at the crowd. Looks at the men with their uplifted hats, at the black-draped horses—Puck is biting Olla in the neck—at the children, and the group of dogs. And all the staring eyes seem to melt into one monster multi-coloured eye, that pierces her through and through; can't they see she is hollow? the fools!

They loosen the hawser and cry all right; and *Bully-boy* swings round, and they steam seaward and she sits and dreams; and the tug dances, and splutters, and fusses through the sunlit sea, past fjord mouths and hamlets, and boats with singing children and yapping dogs, and she never thinks of the future, nor of the steamer she is to meet at the city, nor makes any plan; simply sits and lets her fancies run riot through her tired brain. Sits under a canopy of clear air and listens to the strange conceits that arise in her thinking self. She is a Viking's bond-maid of olden days; she hid on his bark whilst they built up his funeral pyre and laid the old warrior down. She watched them touch the flaming pine knot to his fiery mausoleum, and set him adrift to the strain of a fierce exultant chant of victory, to sail out on his last voyage for a handigrips with the grim foe Death. Ay, he too was a primitive man, with the primæval passions of untamed nature, surging up and eating their way to his soul's core, as restless breakers hollow a place on the coast. And now he is going to rest.

The sun sinks in a superb, audacious blending of hues—orange and scarlet, pink and blue, and lemon-yellow streaks, with splotches of intensest purple, are hurled from a palette of fire in a frenzy of colour. The fishers pause and look curiously at the silent little figure keeping vigil next the flower-decked coffin as she passes them in the pearl-mists of the summer night. Pearl-mists that wrap her in a chilly shroud ; and she fancies that spirit hands spread the canopy of starred blue over them as they glide on ; and the moon peers down and nods to her ; and another moon runs seawards on a shining silver river. And the foam in their wake ripples together like frothing diamond chisps, and the dew falls on the withering flowers, and bathes her pale face, and moistens her dry lips. And the night breeze sings sadly to the thrumming of unseen harps, and soothes her troubled spirit with tender whisperings that only the stricken in soul can catch in snatches from the spirit of nature.

The boy takes the wheel, and the captain brews her some coffee. They have forgotten at the house, in their care for the funeral, to provide her with food or rugs. She is too deliciously weary (there is no new effort either to make unless she chooses) to care. When he brings it to her she swallows it gratefully, and follows him to the stuffy little cabin, and lies down as he suggests, with her head on a pilot coat, and he covers her tenderly with another; she is so small and frail it takes but little. Somehow, it smells 'homey' with its mingled odour of tobacco, and brine, and man, and touches her chilled lone soul like the honest clasp of a warm human hand with a promise of rest and shelter to come; and under its homely spell she falls asleep. And so these two poor human souls, tossed together for good or ill for a brief space, sleep their last together through the summer night. He, to no mortal awakening; she, perchance to a brighter dawn.

List of Books

in

Belles Lettres

Elkin Mathews & John Lane: Publishers and Vendors of Choice & Rare Editions in Belles Lettres.

ALL BOOKS IN THIS CATALOGUE
ARE PUBLISHED AT NET PRICES

1893

Telegraphic Address—
'BODLEIAN, LONDON'

'A WORD must be said for the manner in which the publishers have produced the volume (*i.e.* "The Earth Fiend"), a sumptuous folio, printed by CONSTABLE, the etchings on Japanese paper by MR. GOULDING. The volume should add not only to MR. STRANG'S fame but to that of MESSRS. ELKIN MATHEWS AND JOHN LANE, who are rapidly gaining distinction for their beautiful editions of belles-lettres.'—*Daily Chronicle*, Sept. 24, 1892.

Referring to MR. LE GALLIENNE'S 'English Poems' *and* 'Silhouettes' by MR. ARTHUR SYMONS:—'We only refer to them now to note a fact which they illustrate, and which we have been observing of late, namely, the recovery to a certain extent of good taste in the matter of printing and binding books. These two books, which are turned out by MESSRS. ELKIN MATHEWS AND JOHN LANE, are models of artistic publishing, and yet they are simplicity itself. The books with their excellent printing and their very simplicity make a harmony which is satisfying to the artistic sense.'—*Sunday Sun*, Oct. 2, 1892.

'MR. LE GALLIENNE is a fortunate young gentleman. I don't know by what legerdemain he and his publishers work, but here, in an age as stony to poetry as the ages of Chatterton and Richard Savage, we find the full edition of his book sold before publication. How is it done, MESSRS. ELKIN MATHEWS AND JOHN LANE? for, without depreciating MR. LE GALLIENNE'S sweetness and charm, I doubt that the marvel would have been wrought under another publisher. These publishers, indeed, produce books so delightfully that it must give an added pleasure to the hoarding of first editions.'—KATHARINE TYNAN in *The Irish Daily Independent*.

'To MESSRS. ELKIN MATHEWS AND JOHN LANE almost more than to any other, we take it, are the thanks of the grateful singer especially due; for it is they who have managed, by means of limited editions and charming workmanship, to impress book-buyers with the belief that a volume may have an æsthetic and commercial value. They have made it possible to speculate in the latest discovered poet, as in a new company—with the difference that an operation in the former can be done with three half-crowns.'

St James's Gazette.